A Stash *of* Faith

Trophies of Grace Series
BOOK 2

Betty J Hassler

WESTBOW
PRESS®
A DIVISION OF THOMAS NELSON
& ZONDERVAN

WestBow Press books may be ordered through booksellers or by contacting:

WestBow Press
A Division of Thomas Nelson & Zondervan
1663 Liberty Drive
Bloomington, IN 47403
www.westbowpress.com
844-714-3454

Unless otherwise noted, all Scripture quotations are taken from the Holman Christian Standard Bible®, Used by Permission HCSB ©1999,2000,2002,2003,2009 Holman Bible Publishers. Holman Christian Standard Bible®, Holman CSB®, and HCSB® are federally registered trademarks of Holman Bible Publishers.

Scripture quotations marked (NLT) are taken from the Holy Bible, New Living Translation, copyright ©1996, 2004, 2015 by Tyndale House Foundation. Used by permission of Tyndale House Publishers, Carol Stream, Illinois 60188. All rights reserved.

ISBN: 978-1-6642-7605-5 (sc)
ISBN: 978-1-6642-7606-2 (hc)
ISBN: 978-1-6642-7604-8 (e)

Library of Congress Control Number: 2022915510

Print information available on the last page.

WestBow Press rev. date: 10/09/2023

To those who have shown me
that seeming coincidences are in truth
steps of faith in pursuit of God's redemptive plan.

ACKNOWLEDGMENTS

Standing in our church's fellowship hall, I spotted an older woman carrying a stack of workbooks. At the time, I edited for a major religious publishing house. I recognized the workbooks as resources from our department. I approached her and commented that I was very familiar with that particular workbook.

"Oh, good," she responded. "You can be one of our teachers at the women's jail."

Thus began an almost five year commitment to the jail ministry of First Baptist Church, Nashville, Tennessee. I'd never been in a jail or prison before. I knew nothing of its culture. And I certainly didn't know the laborious process of getting into or out of one. The experience was an eye-opening look into our criminal justice system. I learned that imprisonment doesn't have to have the last word in someone's life.

In *A Stash of Faith*, I've dared to write the story of a prisoner set free by the power of Christ. I don't pretend to have portrayed prison life in its raw reality. I danced around issues that might have offended Christian readers. Any inaccuracies regarding living in a halfway house were written to support the storyline.

My purpose is to tell a true-to-life story of a young man caught in Satan's lies whose transformed life becomes a testimony of how God works in mysterious ways to achieve His purposes. The fun part was tying together the characters from *A Beam of Hope Book 1* to *A Stash of Faith Book 2* in the Trophies of Grace series. I hope their continuing saga will bless you.

My thanks to the publishing team at WestBow Press for their patient indulgence of my imaginary families. And thanks to my *real* family and friends who gave the first drafts their experienced eyes.

May your faith in God's good purposes for you grow in the knowledge that no path is too rocky, no sins too great, and no heart so bruised that God's love can't penetrate and build stronger faith muscles meant to last through eternity.

> When troubles of any kind come your way,
> consider it an opportunity for great joy.
> For you know that when your faith is tested,
> your endurance has a chance to grow.
> So let it grow, for when your endurance is fully developed,
> you will be perfect and complete, needing nothing.
> (James 1:2–4 New Living Translation)

INTRODUCTION

Parker Sloan Hamilton grew up in the wealthy and historic Belle Meade neighborhood of Nashville. Tennessee. A misfit in a family of self-assertive and ambitious people, he lacked the self-confidence of his lawyer father or the regal bearing of his distant mother.

His older sister, Alexis, had been cut from the same upper crust cloth of an elitist family. Parker thought of her as a bully, bossing him into countless sessions of her playacting as a famous fashion designer.

His only source of comfort was his maternal grandmother, Gram Sloan. Unlike the others, she understood his sensitive nature and provided warmth in an otherwise frigid environment.

He attended the prestigious Montgomery Bell Academy right up West End Avenue from his home. His father considered it beneath the family's dignity to graduate one of their children from a public school. Then, as a graduate of Vanderbilt University and Medical School, Parker was well on his way to becoming a world-class surgeon—partly because it was a profession his father could barely stomach (pardon the pun).

Parker would not have known the Brooks family to the east in Green Hills. As newlyweds, Layton and Amy Brooks had bought a simple home on a quiet street off Hillsboro Pike. Soon they welcomed baby Brianne into their loving family. A tragic miscommunication drove them apart when Brianne was three years old.

The story of how Brianne's illness brought the family back together is told in *A Beam of Hope*, the first book in this series. As a result of his own faith journey, Layton began collecting *trophies of grace,* which he displayed inside a large trophy case on the back wall of his man cave. Each trophy named a person and a character trait that served as Layton's spiritual mentors.

How Parker Hamilton's name wound up in that trophy case is a miracle in itself. In fact, how the Brooks and the Hamilton families found themselves in relationship with each other can only be described as an act of God. His good purposes in bringing them together took a very winding and uncertain path when Parker Hamilton found himself in prison.

Spring 1989

Dr. Parker Sloan Hamilton had no warning that today would be the worst day of his life.

With a cup of freshly brewed coffee in one hand and the *Miami Herald* newspaper in the other, he opened the sliding glass door to the balcony of his high-rise apartment. In the distance waves splashed the sandy beach. The beginnings of morning traffic snaked along the coastline.

Settling into his wicker deck chair, he placed the cup on a marbled table and unfolded the paper. Blazoned across the bottom half of the front page a picture stared back at him. Recognizing the face immediately, Parker's pulse quickened. Dino DiMarco had been one of his high-profile facial makeovers.

The article told that a suspect had been caught in a murder for hire scheme. Of course, the name DiMarco appeared nowhere in the story. Other people in the makeover business handled the details of providing new identities and documents for his patients. Parker had only been responsible for creating the new faces.

The cops would still be able to trace DiMarco's real identity through fingerprints. Parker could do nothing about that. What if he or another person turned state's evidence and identified him as the surgeon? What if the district attorney decided to prosecute him? The what-if's made his stomach churn.

Parker hurriedly dressed and drove to work. As he entered the county medical examiner's office, the irony of his workplace wasn't lost on him. He was one of their lead forensic specialists.

Valerie waved from her cubicle. "Hi, Parker, how's it going?" The every morning ritual grated on his nerves this particular day. He nodded and kept going. At six-feet-four, he supposed it would be hard to sneak quietly to his desk. Being voted most eligible bachelor in the mock office pool hadn't helped obscure him. That embarrassing distinction might soon be coming to an end.

Once at his desk, he listened intently to the office chatter that always preceded his workday. Would the DiMarco story make the morning conversation? He felt exposed, as though any coworker passing by would see guilt written all over him.

Trying to distract his thoughts, he checked his e-mail. Who'd been brought in during the night and now awaited his attention on a cold slab in the morgue? The work—gruesome to most of his friends—intrigued him. Now the dark cloud hanging above him left a growing sense of foreboding about his future.

Midday Parker complained to his supervisor of a migraine and begged off early. He drove home in a heavy rainstorm, downed several pills, and waited. For what? He wasn't sure.

South Florida had been a far cry from Boston, where Parker had completed his training in forensic pathology. He'd soon adjusted to the culture if not to the heat. The laid-back mañana philosophy contrasted sharply with his duties in the county medical examiner's office where identifying victims and the nature of their deaths was more than a full-time vocation. Bodies were discovered at all times of the day and night.

Although he loved the excitement of his work, Parker had missed the connection to facial reconstruction that had drawn him to the field of forensic medicine. To scratch that itch he'd become friends with several cosmetic surgeons in the area. Occasionally, he found himself in a consulting role, particularly when a well-known celebrity flew in for a makeover.

One friend in particular, Dr. Brody Colson, had been more than understanding of his need for a few prescription drugs to make it through the day and to relieve his chronic insomnia. He also let him in on a trade secret. "The rich and famous aren't the only ones coming to us for cosmetic surgery," he told Parker. "Some people want to look different for other reasons. Maybe they don't want to be found. They want to disappear for awhile and reappear with a new identity." Brody winked, but Parker simply stared at him in disbelief.

It seemed clear Brody implied these were people with a criminal past or present. They were trying to evade the very law enforcement agencies with whom Parker worked.

Brody continued, "I know what you make in the medical examiner's office. And I know your lifestyle. Soon the two are going to collide. This service pays well. Very well."

Brody was right about finding it hard to live on his meager paycheck. Having grown up in a wealthy Nashville neighborhood, he'd taken the finer things in life for granted. But that was no excuse for engaging in an illicit activity. Parker had reasoned that he could pick up extra income at any of the area clinics or hospitals. Except for his unpredictable hours. How could he schedule even a part-time position?

Parker had the random thought of blowing the whistle on the criminal makeovers, but he decided to keep quiet. Brody knew about his drug habit. That wouldn't look good to his supervisor. He thought consulting on a new look for a few patients was his best option for a little extra cash.

That decision led to assisting with surgeries. Finally, he performed his first solo surgery on a person wanting a makeover. Uncomfortable with the success of the procedure, Parker told himself he' d never do it again. For the hundredth time he weighed his options.

Operating on individuals wanted by law enforcement might be risky behavior, but it was lucrative. And he craved Brody's admiration of his skills. He was solving crimes in the medical examiner's office while moonlighting by surgically altering faces. What irony! To Parker, the nameless criminals were simply limp figures on a gurney attached to an IV tube.

At the time, Parker had wondered what his father would say about the questionable nature of his side job. More than likely, Hollister Hamilton would care more about the potential damage to his own social status and reputation if Parker were caught. As a partner in a prestigious Nashville law firm, Hollister had a certain image to maintain—one that had always superseded concern for his son.

The pills subdued his headache but not the anxiety. Parker waited for his phone, the doorbell, the security desk—some sound to confirm his worst fears. Had he really thought he could get away with surgery on criminals who had lots of money but few places to hide? Was it too late for him to run?

Parker had expected an indictment any day. But to his embarrassment, he was handcuffed while at his office and charged with aiding and abetting criminal activity. The forensic staff witnessed his arrest.

He found little comfort in the fact that Brody Carlson was also behind bars. He made his one phone call to his father, asking him to contact an attorney to get him out on bail.

"Are you serious?" Hollister was in no mood to listen. "After I paid a ton of money for your medical training, you have no collateral? I told you not to take that lousy job. You could have made a fortune right here in Nashville. Now I know why you haven't come begging me for money. If you're going to commit a crime, at least be smart about it." With a snort, he hung up.

Although Hollister had cut every corner of every law imaginable in his effort to win cases before the court, he was unsympathetic toward anyone who got caught. Parker had been careless. That, apparently, was unforgiveable.

Parker curled in a tight ball on the narrow cot in the holding cell, awaiting his hearing later in the day. Knees to his chest, he silently cursed his height.

Despite the clatter of other detainees, he determined not to interact, not even to admit to himself that he was here. Most of his other cellmates lounged on the floor, talking among each other as though they'd met before. A few drunks slept off their hangovers. A couple of guys dressed in suits like him stood along the barred wall lost in their thoughts. None of them seemed to notice his presence or care that he'd joined them.

Eyes closed, images flitted in and out of his dream state. One image kept coming to mind: his exacting father, who even now seemed to hold his son's future in his hands.

"Parker, where are you?" Miss Louisa, the housekeeper, rounded the corner of the formal dining room and entered the foyer with upraised eyes. There sat six-year-old Parker Sloan Hamilton, still as a mouse on the stair landing, peering through the banister rails. "You've got to dress for dinner."

Parker hated dressing for anything, much less dinner. He scrambled to the second floor, then the third, and into the huge storage area that doubled as the attic. His favorite hiding place. Unfortunately, everyone knew it was his favorite hiding place, including Miss Louisa. The housekeeper climbed the stairs and entered the semi-dark room, lighted by a lone window on the side of the house.

"Parker, at my side on the count of three, or I shall fetch Gram Sloan to find you."

The ultimate threat. Parker would rather wear a jacket and tie than disappoint Gram Sloan, his maternal grandmother who lived in a suite of rooms on the second floor. Sure enough, he appeared from behind a sheet-draped armchair and stood before Louisa, only slightly dotted with cobwebs and dust.

Taking his hand, the housekeeper led Parker to his room, where the required clothing had been carefully laid on the bed. "Now, can I trust you to bathe yourself and dress in a timely fashion, or must I treat you as a baby?" she asked.

"No." Parker pulled away from her and started for his bathroom. "I'm not a baby. I'm in first grade."

"Very well, then. I shall return in fifteen minutes. I fully expect you to be ready." She closed the door behind her. Parker stifled a sigh. If she

were in his shoes, she'd resist an appearance at Hollister Hamilton's dining table too.

Louisa's position as housekeeper required her to stand inside the dining room, supervising the serving of guests. In particular, she watched over Master Parker, whose tendency to spill his milk and leave a trail of gravy on the linen tablecloth was well known. He would eventually learn the social graces, although so far little evidence had emerged.

Compounding Parker's natural six-year-old clumsiness was his inability to please his perfectionist father. Tall and imposing, Hollister Hamilton had a military bearing, prematurely gray-streaked hair, and a toned physique. His at-home persona varied little from his legal one. Often, he treated the family as though they were defendants to cross-examine.

Louisa assumed Hollister wanted his son to outshine all others in the ability to parlay verbal assaults and come out the victor. He had the annoying habit of asking Parker what he had learned in school that day and then debating his answer. Parker easily became flustered with his father's courtroom game.

Parker was in a no-win situation. His father's high expectations didn't suit the little boy's personality. Instead of providing a challenge to betterment, his father's provoking seemed to deplete the strength of Parker's ego bit-by-bit.

His mother, Olivia Hamilton, knew better than to cross her husband in front of others. A socially active woman, she kept busy with her memberships on boards of directors and various charities. As Hollister's wife, she had everything material she could want, but she maintained an emotional distance from her husband, children, and admiring public. Like beautifully carved marble, Olivia went about her carefully organized days behind a façade that invited little personal interaction.

Olivia entertained often. While other mothers might have put their children to bed early or fed them in the family dining area when company was present, Olivia was determined to teach her children manners and insisted that Parker and his eight-year-old sister, Alexis, be present.

At dinner the children were seated across from their mother. On this occasion Parker unfolded his linen napkin. Louisa hoped tonight would prove different. Maybe, just maybe, he'd pull out a victory.

The sound of jangling keys and another man noisily stumbling into the holding cell roused Parker sufficiently to remember his surroundings. Some part of Parker's rattled brain wondered why he was dreaming about an incident from his boyhood.

He'd had enough medical training to realize that dreams often held keys to dealing with the past. But why was he reliving this memory now? He'd long ago given up trying to understand his dysfunctional family. Or, had he?

He dreamed because his father still held all the cards. Not just to getting out of jail but also to his sense of self. Back into his dream state, Parker returned to the family drama around the dinner table.

On this particular night Hollister had invited his newest law partner and his wife, Jess and Camilla Burke, to dinner. Hollister had bragged about having lured Jess away from a lucrative lobbying position. While the men talked, Parker busily built a road of green peas through his mashed potatoes. When his father called his name, his arm jerked, sending a forkful of peas flying wildly around him.

As Louisa hurried to collect them, Parker replied nervously, "Yes, sir?"

"Our guest, Mr. Burke, was an Eagle Scout. Show Mr. Burke that new knot you learned at Cub Scouts on Tuesday."

"I-I haven't got a rope."

"Not to worry," his father replied. With flair, Hollister, who had obviously planned to put his son on exhibition, produced a piece of rope from his pocket. Handing it to Parker, he waited in anticipation.

Parker was in a quandary. He had shown his father the knot shortly after arriving home from the scout meeting. That was three days ago, and he hadn't practiced it since then. "I don't think I remember," he began.

"I feel sure you do. You tied it expertly the other night. I certainly wouldn't be asking you to demonstrate a skill you hadn't learned."

"But ..." Parker barely got the word out of his mouth before his father's barrage of recriminations began. Camilla looked silently at her food while Olivia stared without expression at the scene.

Jess broke in, "Hollister, I'm quite sure the boy—"

"The boy," Hollister said with emphasis, "must be taught responsibility. Parker, you may go to your room."

Parker slid out of his chair. As he passed Alexis, she stuck out her foot. Parker was on to her trick and avoided splattering onto the Oriental rug as he had often done. Chin to his chest, Parker mounted the staircase to his room. Louisa collected his plate and silverware as she had at previous functions. Noiselessly, she headed for the kitchen. At the landing Parker wiped a stray tear from his cheek.

"Hamilton, Parker." The burly guard unlocked the gate as he checked his clipboard.

Parker sat up quickly, brushed off his designer suit, ran his fingers through his hair, and followed the uniformed figure down the hall, through several locked doors and cement corridors, and into a small room with a table and four chairs.

At the table sat a thin Latino man with slicked black hair and a shimmering gray suit. Parker had been taught to recognize style. This man reeked of power and money, all the way from his silk pocket handkerchief to his polished Italian shoes.

"Hello. I'm Emanuel Estrada. I'm here to represent you."

No handshake. No eye contact. Apparently, Parker's father had considered the family's reputation and changed his mind. Bail would be posted. Soon he would be back at his apartment, awaiting trial.

Briefly, he wondered what his mother thought of the news, or if his father had even told her? Who else might know? The one person whose opinion of him counted the most now lived permanently with his parents: Abigail Sloan, his maternal grandmother.

Hours later, back in his apartment, having showered and changed into comfortable khaki shorts and a tee shirt, he lay on his leather couch to contemplate his next moves. However, his one consuming thought was a plea to his absent father: *Please don't tell Gram Sloan.* She was on his mind as he drifted back to sleep.

"Come in and say goodnight," Gram Sloan called to Parker as he passed her closed door.

"How did you know I was in the hallway?" he asked as he slowly opened the door . "Do you have a built in radar system?"

"I do," Gram teased, "especially where you are concerned."

"I thought maybe you were asleep." He closed the door behind him.

"Is dinner over already?" She put down the book she'd been reading.

"No, Gram." Parker bowed his head. "Father asked me to leave the table."

"Oh, dear." Gram gathered the child onto her lap and held him close. "Tell me what happened."

Parker recounted the incident. The flying peas almost got a chuckle from his grandmother, but she stifled it as best she could. Abigail Sloan had been warned by her daughter Olivia not to interfere with Hollister's discipline of Parker. But she couldn't simply brush past his wounded feelings. "What do we say when we feel bad?" she quizzed.

"All I need is a little stash of faith in God and in me." Parker had been reciting the phrase since he could talk, thanks to Gram's perceptive grasp of his situation. Jesus' story of the tiny mustard seed was firmly implanted in his mind.

She couldn't let the poor child go to bed hungry. "I have some delicious fruit left from my dinner. How would you like a fruit smoothie for a bedtime snack?"

"Yummy!" he replied, squeezing her tightly. "Gram, you always know how to make me feel better."

"I love you, Parker Hamilton." His grandmother rocked him in her arms. She gently brushed back a damp brown curl from his forehead. "Father, please give my grandson a large portion of Your love," she prayed aloud. They sat entwined for several minutes until she could finally bear to let him go.

Unfortunately, Parker's attorney had little to work with in preparing his defense. Estrada couldn't refute Parker's role in masking the identities of reprobates. Parker felt fortunate to accept a plea bargain to avoid trial.

Surprisingly, his mother and Gram Sloan showed up for the sentencing. Parker figured Gram Sloan had insisted, and Olivia didn't want her traveling alone. Gram's thin frame was bent over as she stood for the judge to enter, but her keen blue eyes held Parker in her gaze.

When the judge handed down a two-year sentence and a year of supervised release, Gram looked at Parker with a sympathetic nod while his mother turned away. He was led out of the courtroom without so much as a goodbye for either.

Parker's sentence of guilty as charged raised quite a stir in his hometown of Nashville. Since the offender was the son of a prominent local attorney, reporters awaited the verdict like lions circling their prey. When they delivered the news to radio and television outlets, the family had no comment.

Hollister Hamilton was too vain to pull his hair out by the roots, but if the effort could have calmed his seething anger, he would have tried. Olivia had come back from Miami a mess. Embarrassed about Parker's ordeal, she had been feigning illness, refusing to entertain or attend functions with him.

He'd soon have to put his foot down. No child of his would ruin all he'd built—and all he lived for. From rural Southern roots, Hollister had joined the army right out of high school and stayed long enough to earn his college degree. Scholarships and student loans paid for law school. Then he took a job as a law clerk in Nashville, the biggest place he had ever lived.

Meeting Olivia, heiress to a horse farm in Kentucky—and eventually marrying her—was by far his greatest achievement. Olivia had the background, the manners, and the looks of a thoroughbred. Together they had produced two children, who he determined would live up to their breeding. Hollister swore that no child of his would ever have to start from as far back in the pack as he had.

Their first child, Alexis, was a girly-girl all into frills and prattle. A show pony, he called her. But his son Parker would be a thoroughbred, just like his mother. Imagine his disappointment when the child couldn't stand up to a fruit fly. Shy, sensitive Parker would have to be prodded and poked to make a man out of him. After all, strict discipline had worked for Hollister.

Parker spent the time between his sentencing and incarceration thinking about his future with a detachment born of disbelief. *This isn't really happening,* he'd tell himself. *I'll wake up tomorrow to the memory of a nightmare.* Only the next day, the nightmare would emerge as reality. His medical license suspended, his career lay in ruins.

He'd heard nothing from Nashville. Not a word from his small cluster of lifelong friends or his family. He could understand silence from Alexis, who was probably unaware of his predicament. She was self-absorbed, as usual, trying to make a name for herself in fashion design.

Another of those swirling memories of the past swept across his consciousness.

"Parker, come to my room. Now." Alexis picked up her sketchbook and moved to the bay windowsill. Her blue eyes flashed between colorless brows

and eyelashes. Although she had the refined look and regal bearing of the Sloan family, her pale coloring gave her an almost ethereal appearance.

Since her room was right across from his, Parker had no way to pretend he didn't hear her. "Aw, I was going to play with my dinosaurs," he griped. He trudged into his sister's room and flopped down on the floor.

"No, come sit over here by the window," she ordered. "I'm going to show you my latest designs."

Parker moved to the spot. Alexis stood a head taller than he did and always seemed to know how to get her way. He wiggled and squirmed as she showed him gowns and cocktail dresses on page after page from her sketchbook. "This one is made of silk," she announced. "What is the difference between silk and chenille?"

"Aw, let me go," he begged. "I don't want to know. What if the guys find out?

"Someday, when I'm a famous fashion designer, you'll be begging to work for me." Alexis closed the book and gave him her haughtiest look. "Father says I'm very pretty and very smart. I'll own a penthouse in New York City, and you will be my butler." She waved him away.

He scrambled to his feet. Parker wasn't sure what a butler did, but nothing could be worse than working for Alexis. In some ways, he felt like he already did.

Parker felt sure Alexis was far enough away not to be affected by his current difficulty. His brother Gavin? Now he was another issue. If Gavin knew about his legal troubles, he would simply laugh at him and make crude remarks. No sympathy there.

Stretching out on the sofa, he thought, *Little bro, how'd you get to be such a lucky brat?*

Olivia Hamilton had been appalled when at age thirty-four, she'd conceived a third child. Her pregnancy had been a well-kept secret until her

fourth month when she shifted to a maternity wardrobe. Even then the subject wasn't discussed around the household, and the children were hardly aware of the life-altering event awaiting them.

Today the household was astir with excitement. Baby Gavin Hollister Hamilton was coming home from the hospital. When the car pulled into the circular driveway in the well-to-do neighborhood of Belle Meade, Louisa and Parker hurried down the stairs to the front door to greet the new arrival.

Hollister helped Olivia out of the front passenger seat while Alexis climbed out of the back. Louisa opened the door on the other side and unbuckled Gavin from his car seat. Dressed in a flowing white gown with blue ribbons, Gavin slept quietly as Louisa carried him into the house.

Standing at the top of the stairwell, Parker announced in a loud voice, "I want to see the baby."

Shush," his mother warned, following Louisa up the stairs with her tiny bundle. In the nursery, Louisa deposited the baby in his bassinet where Parker could get a good look at him.

"He's very little," he observed in a whisper. "Can I see his feet? Can I hold him?"

"Later, dear," his mother said distractedly. "Louisa, call me the moment the baby awakens. I'm going to my room to rest." She moved toward the door. "And Parker is not to be left alone with the baby. Ever! Do you understand?"

"Certainly," Louisa murmured.

With that Olivia started toward her room. Parker continued to stare at the newborn, fascinated by his tiny hands lying across his chest. Parker reached into the crib and stroked them. One small eye peeked at his new surroundings. Gavin wrinkled his forehead and fell back asleep.

"Am I going be a good big brother?" Parker asked Louisa.

"You're going to be a great big brother," Louisa replied, tousling his hair.

5

With time on his hands and plenty of lousy memories to occupy his thoughts, Parker found it familiar territory to review what was certainly one of the most memorable events of his childhood. Gavin's arrival had forever changed the family dynamics.

As the weeks flew by, Louisa took note that Gavin had become a household favorite. Olivia took care of the baby in ways she had rebuffed with the other two—changing diapers, bathing, and dressing the child with considerable interest.

The biggest surprise had been the change in Hollister when he found out this "surprise" was a second son. As hard as he had been on Parker, as unforgiving of minor mishaps and childish misbehavior, he was a different father to Gavin.

As in the situation with Prince Harry of Great Britain, being the "spare" and not the heir gave Gavin a free space Parker never enjoyed. Gavin didn't need to win his father's approval. He already had it.

Alexis' reaction was totally in character. She was thrilled to have another subject in her kingdom. Now eleven, she dressed the baby like she would a doll, exclaiming over each new outfit and taking pride in helping select them. "This would be a good color for Gavin," she would tell the housekeeper. "His complexion needs a darker hue." The youthful fashion designer drew baby clothes along with her ever-growing collection of haute couture.

Parker spent his free time playing in the backyard. Few children lived nearby. His busy parents rarely had time for him to invite friends for a play date. Instead, he chased butterflies on the manicured lawn, caught frogs in Mason jars, waded in the sculpted pool behind their patio, or rode his bike around the front circular driveway.

In the late afternoons he perched on a barstool in the kitchen as Clarissa the cook prepared dinner. There he sampled dishes as though he hadn't already bribed half a dozen cookies from neighboring kitchens in the spacious homes nearby. Parker knew all the household help along the street. They felt sorry for the lonely little boy who waved at them as he passed, knew their names, and listened to their stories from years gone by.

"You're the best cook in the whole neighborhood," he'd tell Clarissa. She'd give him a hug or pat his shoulder. She had to be careful not to show Master Parker the tenderness she felt for the boy. Like Louisa, she'd been warned not to spoil him.

That day, as Parker nibbled a tasty morsel, he wondered aloud, "Clarissa, what good are babies anyhow? Gavin can't do anything." Once Parker discovered that Gavin couldn't play ball or climb trees—much less walk—he'd soon lost interest in the baby.

"You were a baby once, don't you forget." Clarissa wiped at a spot of tomato sauce that had landed on her apron. "I can't believe you're so grown up now."

"I'll be nine in May, right before school is out for the summer." Already the spring rains had produced leafy trees to climb and shrubs to hide behind when Louisa called him to come in from play. Parker's initial enthusiasm for school had waned. He was ready for third grade to end.

"Do you think Gavin will be able to play with me by summer?" Parker asked.

Clarissa pinched his cheek, a habit only she enjoyed. "Honey, let that child be a baby for now. He'll grow up in his own sweet time."

Parker frowned. "Grow up? That's what Father keeps telling me to do. Why does Gavin get to take his time?"

Even at his young age, Parker had determined not to take his feelings out on his younger brother. However, sitting now on his balcony, drink in hand, he mulled over his jealous feelings toward Gavin. He might be all grown up now, but pesky Gavin was living the good life. Instead, he was facing prison time simply for trying to do the same. He hadn't intended life to turn out this way. He'd tried to live up to everyone's expectations. Especially Hollister's.

That fact had been permanently etched in his mind since the night of his sixteenth birthday. He could recall every moment of that disappointing evening.

Standing before the bathroom mirror, he straightened his tie for dinner. He smoothed his brown hair and checked to make sure he didn't need a shave. He frowned when he found his chin to be as smooth as ever. He popped his contact lens into hazel eyes highlighted with long dark lashes that Alexis swore had been stolen from her.

Parker appeared oblivious to the good looks he'd inherited from his mother's family, the Sloans. Gram Sloan said he was lean and lanky like her deceased father, and that pleased him very much. He called her his one-woman cheerleading squad. She said lots of girls had tried to catch his eye. He'd managed to miss all their signals.

Gavin's sudden entrance into his bedroom broke Parker's brief moment of introspection. Panting from his quick trip up the stairs, Gavin breathed, "Dinner's ready. Mom said to come now. Hurry. We're waiting." Then he bounded away as quickly as he had come.

Parker followed him slowly down the stairs. Would his father give him a car as he had done for Alexis on her sixteenth birthday? Hollister hadn't said a word about it. In fact, Parker couldn't remember anyone asking what he wanted. Not even Alexis, who generally expected to be the first to know everything. Alexis had driven home from Moore College of Art and Design in Philadelphia. She'd leave in a couple of weeks for a summer internship in Los Angeles.

As Parker passed the window at the foot of the stairs, he saw Alexis' car parked at the edge of the curved driveway in front of the house. The bright red convertible had the top down as though his sister planned to go out for the evening.

Parker entered the dining room not knowing what to expect. Most of his birthdays had been a letdown. Even when he got what he wanted, the gift was given along with a lecture not to break, leave outside, lose, or otherwise mar it. Tonight everyone was in place as he took his usual seat at the table.

"Well, it seems our birthday boy has arrived. Now we can begin eating," Hollister announced. With that he dipped his spoon into his soup and took a sip. Gavin hummed merrily as he arranged his napkin and picked up his spoon. Parker would never have been allowed to sing at the table. Gavin was a brat, no doubt about it. A spoiled brat.

As usual dinner conversation revolved around Hollister's questions and interests. No one said a word about Parker's birthday, not even Gavin, whose own birthday dinners were noisy affairs with invited guests, followed by the latest entertainment fad. Parker had chosen not to have friends over to witness whatever his embarrassing moment might be, and usually there was at least one. His father saw to that.

After dinner Hollister stood and invited the family to join him as he walked toward the front door. He swung it open with a flourish and beamed at a dark blue sedan parked directly in front of the door on the curved driveway. Silently, he took keys from his pocket and handed them to Parker. Parker stared at the car, then at his father, in disbelief.

"For you." Hollister smiled with satisfaction. He ushered Parker to the driver's side and opened the door. Parker sat on the tan leather seat, looking at the dark wood trim around the dash. Everything about the car screamed "Hollister." Beneath his shirt collar, an angry red hue worked its way toward Parker's face. A car just like Father would drive, he thought bitterly.

But he said exactly what his father wanted to hear. "Th-thank you," Parker stammered. "Thanks for the car."

Silently, Parker put the car into drive and inched it toward a parking place behind Alexis' convertible. There it sat for the rest of the evening, a grim reminder that Parker was not a person to his father. Just a mere extension of Hollister's ego.

6

With only weeks left before reporting to prison, prescription drugs no longer got him through the dreary days and nights. Parker still had friends with connections. He'd looked down on street drugs in the past. Now they were his companions in crisis.

He let out a heavy sigh. How did he ever wind up a druggie?

Parker woke when his head hit the wooden desk with a thump. Startled, he looked at his surroundings. The desk, piled high with medical textbooks and papers, seemed none the worse for having inflicted the rising knot on his forehead.

He stretched and looked for the time: two o'clock. His first exam was scheduled at eight. Getting his MD from Vanderbilt School of Medicine loomed as job one. Slowly, he rose from his chair and wobbled to the small kitchen of his apartment.

Often Parker needed more than caffeine to make it through these all-nighters. He quickly downed two pills—his "study buddies" that helped keep him alert—and headed back to his desk. No more sleep tonight.

The pills were easy to get and gave him an edge, a way to enhance his concentration and energy. Other pills helped him relax—even finally to fall asleep. Although he'd dropped weight and sometimes found his balance or heart rate unsteady, so far so good. He knew he had to monitor drug interactions. After all, he was studying to become a doctor.

Anxiety about graduating in the top ten percent of his class was taking its toll. Parker had little choice but to succeed. His father dangled above his head the money for each semester's tuition and expenses until he reported his class standings.

He knew his father had been deeply disappointed that his son had chosen medicine over law. But Parker had spent about a nanosecond deciding against law as a career. He could never stand before a judge and plead a case. Surely, if he could have, he would have won a few rounds with his father. Besides, medicine gave him a way to distinguish himself from the lawyer in the family, who had never had much use for doctors. In short, his wanting to be a doctor had displeased his father so much that all the labs and long hours were worth it. He grinned at the thought.

All Parker had to do was pass his final exams. He'd already been accepted as a resident at a prestigious medical center in New York City. Meanwhile, Parker was determined to give his best effort. The pills would help him make it through the rest of this week, and then his stress level would drop considerably. At least, he hoped so.

As long as he had access to those pills, he'd be okay.

Occasionally, Parker felt a twinge of guilt about the substances he obtained without a prescription. However, he rationalized that his actions weren't any different from his father's. Hollister had been to every kegger near his college. Besides, he only took drugs occasionally. Really no different than underage drinking.

The fact that he was using them illegally could be a problem if his hypocritical father found out. Well, he'd deal with that if it happened. For now, instead of fighting him in a courtroom with words, Parker would fight with accomplishments in an arena his father couldn't touch. If he needed a little help to bolster his confidence, so be it.

In Parker's clouded mind, his punishment for altering the faces of persons wanted for felonies across the country didn't seem to fit his crime. What about months behind bars was supposed to make him a more law-abiding citizen? Would he emerge from prison a better person? Would prison life offer contact with morally upstanding people?

Hardly. How, then, was prison life going to rehabilitate him? How would it prevent his body from craving drugs? How unpleasant would prison have to be for that to happen? After all, the pills had come along with him to his medical residency.

With his medical degree in hand, Parker moved to a tiny apartment in New York City to begin his residency in reconstructive surgery. Sitting with his laptop resting comfortably in front of him, he clicked the computer screen saver. A review titled "The Applications of Stereolithography in Facial Reconstructive Surgery" appeared. He loved to read about facial reconstruction. His residency would prepare him for specializing in forensic medicine.

Identifying victims through partial remains intrigued his curiosity. Parker grinned at the thought of his father looking at a cadaver. Hollister assumed he'd go into cosmetic surgery and make a mint. Would he ever be surprised to find Parker working in a medical examiner's office someday?

If he could endure the grueling pace of hospital residency, a new future awaited him. He was away from Nashville, away from his father's overbearing presence, his mother's indifference, and the taunts of Alexis and Gavin. He'd learn to manage without Louisa's watchful gaze. She'd helped keep him on the straight and narrow through high school and college with her discreet hints about what might please—or displease—his father.

Living in an apartment off campus for med school had given him more freedom than he'd ever enjoyed and hidden his drug use from everyone, even Gram Sloan. Unfortunately, he'd have few opportunities in coming months to see her. New York was still considered a world away from Nashville. Parker knew his grandmother would keep in touch. The others—he wasn't sure he wanted to hear from them.

7

In his Miami apartment, Parker popped a handful of grapes into his mouth. One fell on the carpet, but he didn't bother to retrieve it. Crumbs from take-out meals pretty well obscured it. He'd had to cut the maid service since he had no discernable income.

The living room was a mess. Papers were scattered everywhere. Discarded cardboard boxes formed a jigsaw puzzle on the coffee table. A couple of lounge pants and several shirts lay across the facing sofa chairs.

Parker paced his apartment. His stash of pills was growing smaller with each passing day. How much longer could he hold out? Anger at his circumstances—an emotion he'd never been allowed to feel in his growing-up years—welled within him. He picked up an empty glass and threw it against the wall.

Freedom from financial worry had been within his grasp! In New York a bright, shiny future stretched before him. One in which Parker would be a heroic figure to victims of horrific accidents and natural disasters. He'd barely been able to contain his excitement when his medical residency began. But his study buddies had come along with him to the Big Apple.

"Dr. Hamilton, Dr. Hamilton to the admitting desk." At first Parker's clouded mind refused to recognize the name as he drifted back to sleep. However, the blaring emergency room intercom was hard to ignore.

His entire body felt as though he'd been dragged through a row of thorn bushes. Joints and muscles ached. His head throbbed. Pushing through the fatigue, Parker grabbed two pills from his pocket and downed them without water. Making his way to the admissions desk, he looked over the information the nurse handed him and entered the room of the accident victim. After a quick exam, Parker prepped for emergency surgery.

The high he felt when operating wasn't drug induced. The thrill of being needed—having a highly-regarded skill to bring to the situation—and the challenge of not only saving a life but preventing permanent disfigurement—topped any feeling he'd ever imagined. Parker quickly took his place beside the figure on the gurney.

Afterward, Parker made his way back to the doctor's lounge. He settled into a massive recliner, and pulled the lever, shooting his feet into the air. His racing mind wouldn't quit. He tried to drift off but strange images and the ever-present sensitivity to hearing his name called kept him from sleep. Minutes later Dr. Nicholas Lochland came whistling into the room. His white jacket, blonde hair, and pale coloring made him a ghost-like apparition in Parker's troubled haze.

"Hey, Parker. Wake up." The doctor headed for the window and turned the blinds, revealing the gray morning light. Parker mumbled something incomprehensible and tried to ignore him.

Dr. Lochland seemed to take diabolical pleasure in tormenting the sleep-deprived residents, probably revenge from his own residency. He could be a sympathetic figure, since he squirreled Parker's prescription drugs from the hospital pharmacy. But he also expected the pills to do their work. He had no compassion when young doctors tried to rest on hospital time.

"Get up, my good man." The doctor flipped the lever of the recliner, jolting Parker upright. "It's time to make rounds."

Residency completed, Parker left for Boston to practice with renowned reconstructive surgeon, Dr. Jerome Andropolos. At last, no more routine surgical procedures and emergency room operations.

With awe, like an apprentice to the master, Parker assisted Andropolos in transforming children with facial deformities, adult burn and accident victims, and those flown in by international disaster relief agencies. The charity work was his favorite, although it meant extra-long hours on his "off" time.

The Christmas holidays provided an opportunity to leave cold, snowy Boston for the relative warmth of Nashville. Christmas itself meant almost nothing. Mostly, he wanted to see Gram Sloan.

After a lavish family dinner in their Belle Meade mansion, the family settled in his father's study for drinks. Gram Sloan played a role in getting a begrudging compliment out of her son-in-law. "Hollister, did you by chance see the article about Dr. Andropolos in the paper recently?"

"No, I must have missed it." Hollister sipped his gin and tonic.

"The Tennessean *reported his groundbreaking work in rebuilding the face of a well-publicized crime victim. Parker, didn't you assist with the surgery?"

"Yes." Parker looked uncomfortable. Would his father quibble over the details, interrogating him like a witness on the stand? Hollister reluctantly acknowledged his pride in Parker's achievements. Louisa beamed her approval while Olivia nodded graciously. Alexis and Gavin were too much into themselves even to notice.

Later, Parker enjoyed a relaxing moment on Gram's couch in her suite. "Thanks for the compliment about the article."

"You deserve more than that," she affirmed and brushed off his gratitude with a wave of her hand. "I'm very proud of you." Gram looked him over intently. "There is something that worries me, however."

As she moved from her chair to a place beside him on the couch, he avoided her gaze. "Parker, you don't look well. I'm not sure what I'm sensing. Are you taking care of yourself?"

Fighting the urge to retreat quickly to his room, he had to stick it out. That would make her more suspicious. "Gram, you know how us single men eat. Every short-order cook in Boston knows me by name."

Her laugh assured him he had temporarily put her fears to rest. He pecked her cheek and hastily said goodnight. In his bathroom he opened a container and quickly popped two pills into his mouth. As water trickled down his throat, he headed for his laptop and quickly maneuvered to one of his favorite websites. The field of forensic facial reconstruction was burgeoning. Would he soon have a job in his chosen vocation?

On a stormy December day Parker began his sentence at a prison in central Florida. He had failed the drug test given as part of the admission process. Street drugs had been his guilty secret, known only to his suppliers, but now his illegal habit was on record.

Parker's first few days passed in the haze of drug withdrawal. Once clean—though not by choice—he realized drugs wouldn't be hard to find in prison. He made the decision, mostly out of fear, not to use them. He could endure two years of confinement. Maybe less if he stayed clean. But not a day more.

Thoughts of punishment or more time behind bars scared him into compliance. More than living without drugs temporarily was the fear of lengthening his sentence. He needed to play by the rules, do what it took to maintain a clean record. He wasn't street smart; prison guards seemed to easily sniff out guys like him. After all, getting out was the only goal left to him. His other goals lay in ash heaps around him.

Reality smacked him in the face. Parker missed even the smallest aspects of freedom—the ability to turn a light off or on, to choose his own clothing, to shower in privacy. Getting from the cellblock to any other part of the facility involved a Herculean effort of gaining permission, waiting for an escort, and waiting even more before being escorted back. Often, time away from the cellblock seemed hardly worth the effort.

Parker also had to learn the culture into which he had been thrown. Cellies competed to see who could be the toughest, rudest, or most indifferent. In Miami Parker had become accustomed to a bit of prestige. Here, he felt like a target. Never good at defending himself, he was a source of ridicule. Everything from his manners, to his education, to his Southern drawl provided amusement to the coarse men around him, most of whom had grown up in rough neighborhoods.

A cellie named Jorge imitated him unmercifully. "Hey, guys, did you hear Parker talk to that guard? 'No, sir, thank you very much, sir. And would you like that with sugar, sir?'" Jorge pranced through the common area with an effeminate swagger. Everyone let loose with catcalls.

Parker grimaced and thought of a few choice swear words. Was it his fault he'd been taught to respect authority? He cursed his father for insisting on no talking back: yes sir and no sir were absolute, unyielding rules.

Gradually, Parker learned how to go along and get along. Some of what that cost him left him ashamed. He could picture Gram looking at him from a corner of the room. The desire to hide from her penetrating eyes engulfed him as he lay on his lumpy cot.

Nights were a mishmash of insomnia and dark dreams. What had he gotten himself into? And how would he get himself out? Already cut off from everything he knew, even Gram's letters reminded him of his isolation.

Months after his incarceration, Parker's situation finally sank in: his career in forensic medicine was over. Professionally and personally at his lowest level, Parker fell into deep depression. The inmates' teasing mostly ended. Parker no longer responded.

Tomorrow Parker would graduate from the prison's drug education program. A certificate of completion would be placed in his prison file. Then he'd obligingly attend a recovery group to keep up his fake resolve to abandon drugs.

This irony wasn't lost on Parker. He needed a clean record of compliance to reduce his prison sentence. However, he craved drugs to relieve the monotony of his life. He needed escape from his meaningless present.

Now the lights in his cellblock were out. Snores emanated from surrounding bunks. But sleep would be a long time coming. Without the pills, his insomnia had sprung into high gear. Once out of prison, he knew he'd do whatever it took to get the drugs again.

"Get up! Out of the way." The guard pushed and prodded until Parker groaned, stumbled to his feet, and stepped aside. A new cellie climbed to the bunk above his. Parker could tell it was almost daybreak, but he had no stomach for introductions. He fell back onto his mattress and went back to sleep. Hours later, he felt the shaking from the bulky weight of someone climbing down from overhead.

"Hey, man, I'm Malcolm. Looks like you're my closest cellie." The man laughed as though he'd told a funny joke. By the time the breakfast trays were cleared, Parker had heard his life story. Malcolm had grown up around the docks of Miami, fallen into the wrong crowd, and been convicted of extortion. All he had left in the world was a mother with terminal cancer. Soon, everyone in the cellblock had heard Malcolm's story. No one had heard his.

Despite their differences, Parker found it hard to dislike Malcolm. He proved to be friendly and showed respect. Unlike Parker, he actually seemed interested in the men around him. Since he bunked above him, the two could hardly have avoided each other. But Parker made it clear he wanted his space.

At least on Tuesday and Thursday nights Malcolm was out of the cellblock attending chapel services or a Bible study. At first Parker was baffled by the idea. Then he found it funny. Religious services in prison? The thought had never crossed his mind.

Like Parker, Malcolm received a lot of teasing from the other cellies. But unlike Parker, Malcolm didn't seem fazed by it. As a matter of fact, he took it with good humor, occasionally poking fun at himself. "You think I go to chapel for the thrill of it?" he'd ask. "Why, I'd have to go twice a day for the rest of my life to outdo my bad."

Then Malcolm would launch into his story about finding Christ at a dock ministry aimed at rescuing youth gang members. Unfortunately, by then he'd already committed the crime that eventually landed him in prison. After a few retellings of Malcolm's story, the other cellies backed off. Who wanted to hear that Jesus nonsense again? A smart defense, Parker thought with amusement. Maybe I should have tried that angle?

One evening Malcolm came back from chapel especially pumped about what had happened. Mildly curious, Parker asked Malcolm to describe the service.

"Did you ever go to church?" Malcolm asked.

"Yeah, as a kid. You know, it meant a lot to my father's image." Parker chuckled thinking about Hollister in church. The formal ritual of the services generally put his father to sleep. Olivia would elbow him awake, then the process would repeat. Alexis would draw while Parker played with his fingers, shuffled his feet, or made small sounds with his throat. Louisa, dutifully sitting behind them, would find that soft spot on his shoulder muscle. Church was literally a pain in the neck.

Parker found it hard to imagine voluntarily going to church. As a matter of fact, he hadn't been in church since Gavin's christening. Soon after the event, the entire family had stopped attending. Olivia said it was simply too taxing to get three children ready in time for the services.

This irony wasn't lost on Parker. Somehow three children were dressed and fed by seven o'clock on weekdays, but the family couldn't manage to get in a car and drive to church by eleven o'clock on Sundays. Church obviously didn't mean very much to the Hamiltons back then, and it certainly didn't mean anything to Parker in his present circumstances. Parker had declined Malcolm's frequent invitations.

However, Malcolm's enthusiasm for each service never waned. During the evenings while cellies fought over television channels, he read his Bible. Nothing in Malcolm's noisy and sometimes violent surroundings deterred his spiritual activities. Bedtime would find him kneeling on the hard concrete floor to pray before climbing up to his bunk. Strange, Parker thought. Malcolm may think he has God on his side, but it looks like we've wound up in the same place.

Working in the prison sign shop wasn't the worst job he could have. Poor Malcolm was stuck in the mess hall cleaning up after everybody. But the everyday routine left too much time for him to think.

Why did it seem he was obsessed with reviewing his life history? Mundane incidents from his childhood and youth certainly played no role in his incarceration. Or did they? Was he set up to fail? Or did he fail through willful choices? And what difference would the answer ultimately make?

He hated the role of pretend therapist, rehashing the past to find clues to his present. Yet some force compelled him to go back to places and events he'd just as soon forget. This introspection wasn't like him. It wasn't like him at all. Too much of his life had been spent following rote commands, trying to stay out of anyone's crosshairs, especially his father's.

After work, he hung out in the prison library as much as possible. But unlike those cramming to find a loophole in whatever law they had broken, or the few studying for a GED or taking college courses, he had no goals to pursue. The banal fiction, self-help books, and biographies didn't interest him. Dusty law books reminded him too much of his father.

One evening Parker lay on his bunk while most of the cellies watched a mindless sitcom on television. Malcolm was in the bunk above him reading—probably something religious. Bored, he let out a frustrated sigh.

"Did you say something?" Malcolm asked from the top bunk.

Startled, Parker almost hit his head on the frame above him. "No," Parker snarled.

"Thought I heard something," Malcolm explained. "Sorry."

Parker's foul mood intensified. "Some of us don't live in a world of people in bathrobes and beards who think they've found all the answers. Life is a crock, man. Might as well get used to it."

Malcolm didn't say anything, which made Parker even madder. "What's with you?" he fairly shouted at the thin mattress and springs separating them.

"Come and see," Malcolm replied in an even voice. "Chapel is tomorrow night."

Was it boredom, anger, or curiosity? Parker didn't know. But for some reason, he agreed to go with Malcolm to chapel. He knew he could make mincemeat of Malcolm's religious beliefs, but he wanted to scope out the place first. Get a feel for what happened there.

The chapel services were always crowded with men looking for diversion or inspiration or something to fill the vast emptiness in their lives. Some came to mock, but chapel eventually made them uncomfortable, and their efforts at disrupting the gatherings weren't tolerated.

Chaplain Jacob Thomas met Parker the first night he visited. Later, Parker would learn that Chaplain Jake, as the cellies called him, knew every returnee by name and greeted each of them with warmth and interest. Although the leaders of the chapel services varied by denominational labels, Chaplain Jake dropped by frequently and led special services himself.

The chaplain trained all the volunteers who led Bible studies in the various cellblocks or preached at the chapel services. Occasionally, he counseled inmates privileged enough to leave their cells for a short visit to his office. He also had the sad duty of informing inmates when relatives died, helping them make arrangements if they were allowed to attend the funerals.

At that first chapel service, Parker shook the chaplain's hand uncomfortably and mumbled his name, quickly moving on to sit next to Malcolm toward the back of the room. Later, as Parker lay on his bunk, he tried to reconstruct what happened. The service seemed a blur—so different from the liturgical routines of the only church he'd attended.

The men raised their hands, shouted out "amen" and words of praise, and sang unfamiliar songs at the top of their lungs. Parker watched as Malcolm seemed transfixed by the music, then lifted his hands in prayer.

Someone preached, but Parker's mind kept wandering. Why did he feel so out of place? What was Malcolm getting from these experiences that seemed to set him apart from the others?

After the men returned from chapel to their cellblocks, Parker was disappointed that Malcolm didn't ask him what he thought about the service. He had come up with several clever replies to questions Malcolm was sure to ask.

The following week, due largely to Malcolm's strategy of silence, Parker attended the next chapel service. *I'm just curious,* Parker told himself. Just trying to find out what makes Malcolm tick. After the service, Parker was exiting alongside the others when Chaplain Jake motioned to the escort guard to go on without Parker. "Come back for him in about fifteen minutes," the chaplain directed.

Immediately Parker's antennae shot up. Nervously, he sat in a chair on the back row. Sitting across from him, the chaplain tried to make small talk, but Parker wasn't buying in. Although Chaplain Jake seemed well meaning and easygoing, to Parker he was part of the prison establishment, an establishment he detested.

"What's your religious background?" the chaplain asked amiably. After establishing that Parker had very little, the chaplain smiled. "I thought Nashville was the buckle of the Bible belt."

"That description escaped my attention," Parker replied evenly.

"So what brought you to attend chapel services?" the chaplain queried. "Simple curiosity and boredom," Parker said with emphasis.

Chaplain Jake seemed to take his responses in stride. When the fifteen minutes were up, Parker left for his cellblock feeling the victor. No way would this religious nut penetrate his defenses.

10

During the ensuing weeks, Parker attended chapel frequently, although he deliberately missed a few services so as not to appear too interested. Parker had never owned a Bible, much less read one. The chapel services, and the way the Bible's message seemed to affect most of the regulars, intrigued his intellectual curiosity. If the Bible were true, why hadn't Parker heard more about it growing up? And what kind of hold did it seem to have on so many people?

His cellie was a case in point. Malcolm had fallen under the Bible's mysterious spell. He seemed to have come to grips with his criminal past and longed for a different future. Instead of Parker's inner rage, Malcolm had a peace about him.

Parker couldn't dismiss the obvious differences between Malcolm's approach to the other cellies and his own. Malcolm cared about the men. No matter what had brought each one to this awful place, Malcolm saw potential in every face and offered hope beyond their present circumstances. Although Parker wasn't familiar with the biblical meaning of the word *grace*, he grasped the fact that Malcolm viewed each inmate as having value, even though all of them were lawbreakers.

Eventually Chaplain Jake coaxed Parker into signing up for a small group Bible study, conveniently in Parker's cellblock. The chaplain would lead it himself, a rare occurrence considering his many duties. Malcolm was the first to sign up for the class. When Parker agreed to attend, Malcolm gave him a playful jab on the shoulder, finally acknowledging Parker's newfound spiritual interest.

Days later Chaplain Jake gave Parker his first Bible—even inscribing it with a personal note. Reading was one of his favorite pastimes, so Parker plunged in with fervor to study the Book of Mark, the subject of the new class. As he read, he found himself asking Malcolm questions. Where did this fellow Jesus come from? Why did God call him His Son? If these were good people, why did John the Baptist wind up in prison?

The stories of Jesus' life, parables, and miracles touched Parker at a deep level. Then, in Mark 8:36–37 Parker read Jesus' baffling question, "What does it benefit a man to gain the whole world yet lose his life? What can a man give in exchange for his life?" At present Parker's life meant little. Could Parker really exchange his meaningless life for one of value?

When Jesus said in Mark 9:37, "Whoever welcomes Me does not welcome Me, but Him who sent me," Parker stopped reading. An outlandish claim, Parker reasoned. Jesus apparently believed it. So did the disciples. Unlearned men, steeped in the tradition of a coming Messiah, spread this tall tale. Certainly they couldn't be trusted. Parker felt badly for Malcolm who'd bought into the fantasy. Still, something had turned Malcolm's life around.

The next day Parker showed up for the first session of Chaplain Jake's Bible study without being reminded. Parker reasoned that with his education and obvious mental abilities, he could take down these yokels in one hour. The first class hadn't even begun, but Parker was more skeptical than ever.

Unfortunately, Parker's mental gymnastics failed to convince Chaplain Jake or the other believers who attended the study. Undaunted, Parker kept coming to the sessions, kept wrestling, kept pointing out his perceived inconsistencies in Jesus' story. Those in the class pounded back with their love and patience. They smiled as he stormed. They responded patiently as he railed. Finally, he gave up his arguments and sat in stony silence.

When the chaplain assigned chapter 15, Parker read with alarm Jesus' conviction as a result of shoddy trials. Parker knew enough about the law to see through the Pharisees' schemes. No one—not even this Jesus— deserved to die by crucifixion. Then in verse 39, the centurion saw how he died and confessed, "This man really was God's Son!"

The centurion's statement kept repeating itself, tumbling through his mind as he slept. In his waking hours, the skeptic in him wrestled. The very idea that one man's actions on one day in history could mean anything to Parker's present circumstances solidified his disbelief.

The following week Parker's Bible study took him to Mark chapter 16, the part about Christ's resurrection. As he lay on his bunk, he felt heat spreading across his cheeks. *Am I supposed to accept the resurrection as a real historical event? The whole book of Mark is a sham,* he concluded. *How could anyone believe this tripe?* He spewed a barrage of curse words toward the ceiling and slammed the Bible against the nearest wall.

At the next group session Chaplain Jake began by offering several observations that would support the resurrection claim. As he talked, the scowl etched between Parker's eyebrows began to soften. Was it possible that Jesus had, indeed, risen from the dead?

More than 400 witnesses had claimed to see the risen Jesus, including His disciples. The guards at the tomb had been bribed to keep silent about why they had not stopped the supposed theft of the body. Jesus' body was never found. None of the supposed witnesses had recanted their story.

Even secular history had produced no plausible explanation for the resurrection miracle. The idea that Jesus had never really died seemed farsical since the two men crucified with him had died. Trickery of any kind—swapping out the bodies or making up the entire tale—could never be proven. The resurrection of Jesus was either a historical event or the biggest swindle in recorded history.

Chaplain Jake concluded, "Our next Bible book study will further affirm the reason Jesus was destined to die and be resurrected "from the beginning of time." Parker decided to stick it out.

The Bible study group finished the book of Mark and plunged into the theologically deep waters of the first chapter of the book of John. Chaplain Jake said the book was a different take on the life of Christ, a life that now intrigued Parker more than he cared to admit. Parker had read and reread the chapter, trying to untangle and absorb the absurdity that Jesus pre-existed with God from the beginning of time.

Chaplain Jake quoted Genesis 1:1. "In the beginning God created the heavens and the earth." He said everyone should know that verse by heart.

In his childhood, Parker had only heard Gram Sloan speak of God as creator. All his teachers and professors in science classes, not to mention his medical school faculty, had argued against a supreme being. They had impeccably laid out their cases: macro- and microevolution explain all we need to know about the origins of life. Or did they? What if his mentors were wrong?

Parker wondered what God—if He existed—had to do with his past, present, and future. If God created him for some specific purpose, why was he stuck behind these concrete walls and barbed wire?

The group had just begun John chapter 2 when a new member joined their ranks. Malcolm had recruited Ike and apparently saw in him some quality Parker couldn't fathom. Ike was street-smart with a thick waist and jowls that would be the envy of any bulldog. His disposition, however, was more akin to a stereotypical pit bull.

Ike seemed intent on arguing his narrow interpretation of the Bible. Parker watched with interest as Malcolm interacted with Ike. Words that should have irritated Malcolm to the core seemed to roll off him. Although Malcolm was quick to mentally joust with Ike over the Scripture's meaning, something more important was taking place between them. Malcolm's interest in Ike was undeserved. Nothing about Ike invited affection. Yet Malcolm cared about him. And he cares about me, Parker admitted—like no one else, except for Gram Sloan.

As they continued their study, Parker recognized Malcolm's approach as similar to the one Jesus used with Nicodemus in John 3, the woman at the well in John 4, and the invalid at the pool in John 5. His only motive appeared to be love (*For God loved the world*) and He exuded compassion (*You will never thirst again*). However, Jesus challenged the beliefs and suppositions of those He met (*Do you want to get well?*).

Parker found himself mentally defending Jesus during the trade-offs between Malcolm and Ike. Strange, since Parker had never professed belief in any part of the Bible. Strange, indeed!

Unfortunately for Parker, Malcolm received word that his request for a transfer to a prison in South Florida had come through. He wanted to be closer to his ailing mother. She hadn't been able to make the long trip to central Florida, and he feared he might never see her again. Malcolm gave Parker a bear hug before he left, promising to pray for him.

Parker's next bunkmate, Ralph, was an abrasive man, who showed no interest in the Bible study or spiritual things. Like a prickly porcupine, he bristled at every provocation. His verbal abuse soon convinced Parker to leave him alone. Without Malcolm, Parker felt more isolated than ever.

In addition, a new guard in his cellblock seemed to take persistent delight in making his life even more difficult. Officer Burrows didn't appreciate Parker's refined manner and education, even delaying his efforts to go to chapel services until it was too late to attend.

Where is this God that Malcolm kept talking about? The one who cares about me? he wondered. Chaplain Jake tried to encourage him. Yet, his attempts at belief hung in mid-air.

One thing Parker's isolation allowed for was reading, and he devoured the Bible. When Parker had first opened it, he'd approached it as though it was a poisonous snake crawling through his hands. He'd assumed unlearned men pieced it together with an agenda: to convince the world that their brand of truth was the only legitimate way to God. Obviously, his scholarly knowledge would preclude his falling for the Bible's mix of folklore and superstition.

Although some of the Bible left him wondering, he gradually absorbed the repeating saga: God's love spared His people from calamity; they rebelled and turned to idols; God punished them; they returned to God, only to fall prey to their own sinfulness once again. Yet God continued to rescue them.

Try as he might, Parker couldn't dismiss the story of God's love for all people. Did that love include him? The possibility that Parker had a Father who loved him felt overwhelming. One night, while the other cellies watched a beauty pageant, Parker fell to his knees by his bunk and cried his heart out.

Cheeks wet with tears, Parker knew in his heart he wanted to be a believer. The decision wasn't so much an event as a progression of events. He'd watched it occur as if in a distant body floating above him. Parker couldn't resist the irresistible love of Jesus, demonstrated in a Bible study group of guilty sinners saved by grace. What was happening to him? Where was the anger, the hopelessness? Despair was turning to desire. Was a new kind of light dawning? Was new life possible?

He stayed after chapel one night to approach Chaplain Jake privately. "I can't reason my way out of this feeling," Parker admitted. "I'm drawn to this Jesus in a way I can't comprehend. What's going on?"

"You're right," he replied. "Jesus is drawing you into His kingdom. But first, you must accept His offer of salvation." The chaplain explained that Jesus died for Parker's sins, and Jake's too. God accepted Jesus' sacrifice for sin, and now Parker had the opportunity for a life of forgiveness and relationship with His true Father, God.

Parker prayed The Sinner's Prayer as Chaplain Jake said each phrase.

Dear God, I know that You love me. I admit I am a sinner.
Please forgive me for my sin. I place my faith in Jesus Christ
who paid for my sins, and I claim Him as the Lord of my
life. Thank You for saving me and giving me eternal life with
You in heaven.
In Jesus' name I pray, Amen.

Once more tears streamed down his cheeks. A strange sense of wholeness and peace filled the cavern of his soul. The brothers in Christ—a chaplain and a cellie—embraced. Due only to the grace of a merciful God, Parker left the chapel and headed back to his cell—a new man in Christ.

12

The following day Parker did something he'd never even thought of doing in all his months of incarceration. He made a phone call.

"Hi, Gram. It's Parker calling from Florida. How are you?"

Gram cleared her throat a couple of times. Parker recognized her habit of clearing her thoughts as well.

"Well ... hello, dear. I must say I'm surprised to hear your voice."

"Yes ma'am. I'm sorry I haven't called before. I've got good news."

"Oh, my. Are they releasing you early?"

"No. I wish. But I've got better news than that. I've become a believer."

"A believer in what, dear? I'm sorry, I guess I'm just so surprised to hear from you. Tell me all about it."

Parker spent the next few minutes explaining about Malcolm and Chaplain Jake and the Bible study. He ended with, "I've given my life to Jesus."

He listened for a response but only heard sniffles coming across the phone line. "Gram, are you all right?"

"Oh, yes. Better than that. I've prayed for this day ever since you were born. You've made me the happiest grandmother on the planet."

Knowing his phone minutes were almost up, he quickly ended the conversation with, "All I need is a little stash of faith in God and in me." He imagined he could see, if not hear, Gram's contented smile.

In the days and weeks after giving his life to Christ, Parker found fellow believers all around him. Faces in the chapel auditorium were no longer a blur but friends playing ball in the rec area, cleaning the mass of hallways, or working near him in the prison sign shop.

He prayed his first faltering prayers, offering his thanks for lifting the burden of despair and low self-esteem that had plagued him for as long as he could remember. He promised to seek purpose and fulfillment in God's plans for his life, not his own.

Someday soon, Parker hoped to thank Malcolm for the role he had played. Malcolm kept in touch with the chaplain, who had offered to be his mentor. Soon to be released, Malcolm hoped to begin a street ministry in Miami. Now Parker had his first intercessory prayer request: *Lord, give Malcolm your protection and provision.*

Late one afternoon Parker was shooting hoops in the rec area when he spotted Ike leaning against the fence enclosure. Ike had dropped out of the Bible study group soon after Malcolm left for south Florida. Parker thought he should at least invite him back.

"Hey, Ike," Parker shouted, ambling toward the fence. Ike stared at him with lifeless eyes, lost in a haze all too familiar to Parker. *He's using!* Parker felt his heart rate climb. He looked around, but no one was paying them any attention. Ike slumped to the ground as the only peace he knew took him to a short-lived fantasyland far beyond the prison grounds.

Parker breathed the phrase he'd learned in chapel: "There but for the grace of God go I." Ike was physically in prison, but he was also chained by the confinement of addiction. Although he had argued his firmly held religious tenets with Malcolm in the Bible study, those beliefs hadn't set him free.

Early one morning a guard shook Parker awake. "Get your clothes on and come with me." Now accustomed to orders with few instructions, he struggled into his clothes. Moments later a surprised Parker found himself in Chaplain Jake's office. *What's the chaplain doing here so early in the morning?* he wondered.

The two men shook hands and Parker slumped into the chair across from his desk, still blinking the sleep from his eyes. Solemnly, the chaplain said, "I've been asked to notify you of your Grandmother Sloan's death near midnight last evening." Parker sat stunned. Gram Sloan's letters—his only contact with home—had become rare as her health declined. Still, he hadn't contemplated losing her so soon.

"I was told she passed peacefully. Do you want me to arrange for you to attend the service?"

Parker considered the possibility. All he could think of was the last conversation he'd had with his father when he'd slammed the phone down in disgust. He couldn't face Hollister Hamilton, nor did Parker have any reason to think any of the rest of the family wanted to see him.

Finally, Parker replied, "No, I don't want to be a distraction. I'll write Mother a note." Slowly, he rose and walked back to his cellblock, now filled with the noise of cellies dressing for work.

A tiny ray of hope had died along with his Gram. Would Parker ever see his family again? But, then, why would he want to? He'd lost the person who meant most to him. He was so grateful Gram knew about his becoming a Christian. But he regretted his failure to ask her for forgiveness for the hurt he'd caused her along the way.

Christ would make all things new one day. He'd see Gram again, and their joy would be unbelievable. Meanwhile, Parker had to trust the Lord's wisdom in this present sea of darkness.

Gram Sloan's death uncovered deep emotions within him that had lain buried, hidden even from him. The grief seemed unbearable. Why would a loving Savior give him a new life only to take away his only hope in a hopeless situation, his one comfort in a comfortless place? Parker would have gladly traded his life for Gram's. If only he could have been the one to die.

Startled, Parker paused mid thought. Could Jesus love me so much that He had willingly traded His life for mine?

He let the thought sink in. Jesus had done just that for him.

Parker reflected on all he had accomplished in life—and all he had lost. A phrase from a song often selected for chapel services played in his mind. "At the cross … for sinners such as I." He bowed his head and heaved sobs of remorse for his ungratefulness. Thanks to Chaplain Jake, Parker was beginning to understand more fully what dying had cost Christ: temporary separation from His heavenly Father.

Several weeks after Gram's death, Chaplain Jake began a sermon series that would culminate in the Easter chapel service. The chaplain was more than aware of his captive audience when he reminded them that believers are "prisoners of Christ."

Preaching from Galatians 4:1-7 Chaplain Jake explained that mastery by Christ set us free from the slavery of sin. Now believers are adopted sons of God, heirs of all of Christ's riches in glory. Paul wrote in Galatians 5:1, "Christ has liberated us into freedom. Therefore stand firm and don't submit again to a yoke of slavery."

Chaplain Jake went on to explain that this freedom came with responsibilities. "Don't use this freedom as an opportunity for the flesh, but serve one another through love. For the entire law is fulfilled in one statement: Love your neighbor as yourself" (Galatians 5:13-14).

Parker couldn't help but think of Malcolm, whose love for his fellow cellies stood in stark contrast to all the others around him. What would it mean for him not just to love others but to serve them as well? Now he had a new Master, one whose kingdom required first allegiance (Matthew 6:33). Although Parker still had plenty of questions about the Christian life, he had tried the other end of the spectrum.

Parker couldn't deny his relationship with his heavenly Father or how it filled the void in his life. In a paradoxical way, Parker had both found a new kind of freedom and yet lost the old one. Lost the illusion of self-control and self-determination. Lost it to the authority of his new Master.

If he were truly a servant of Christ, what would that look like once he was out of prison?

13

Thoughts of Gram Sloan continued to fill Parker's mind as he worked at the prison sign shop, ate in the noisy cafeteria, and tried to shut out the endless barrage of television sitcoms in the common room of his cellblock.

His newly found faith hadn't kept this place from being a prison. The men around him still cursed and taunted, stole from his meager supply of toiletries, and quite literally tripped, bumped, bruised, and occasionally threatened him with serious bodily harm. No one could believe he wasn't selling or buying drugs. Most of the gangs were in another part of the building, walled away from the less violent prisoners. Yet his cellmates were, after all, still criminals.

Following the example of Malcolm, he'd tried telling them about the difference Christ made in his life. So far, he'd had no takers. His shyness and lack of people skills made it harder than he felt it should be. However, he didn't have long to practice his witnessing training. Soon he'd be eligible for the federal supervised release program, mandated by the judge at his sentencing.

One afternoon Parker's attorney, Emanuel Estrada, met with him across a desk in the visitor's area to explain more about the federal program. As he gathered documents into his briefcase, he warned, "You could find yourself back here in a nanosecond if you so much as look at a non-physician ordered prescription drug or any type of illegal drug—not to mention altering faces. Don't forget, your license to practice medicine has been suspended."

Parker averted his lawyer's eyes, shook his hand, then followed the guard out of the visitor's area and back toward the cellblock. On the way Parker saw Chaplain Jake walking toward him.

"Might have some news for you soon," Parker called, trying to be as mysterious as possible in a place of few secrets.

"Might have some for you." The chaplain grinned. "I'll set up a time for us to talk."

Several days later Parker found himself in Chaplain Jake's office, settled in one of the very few upholstered chairs to be found in the prison. Although worn and faded, the chair was a special luxury in a building full of bare wood and metal.

Chaplain Jake had a surprising announcement. The chaplain had found a Christian halfway house in Orlando willing to accept Parker as a resident for six months. The chaplain explained its rules and regulations.

"You'd be in a controlled environment," he said. "And one that promotes a godly lifestyle. I see obvious benefits. I hope you do, also."

Parker mulled over his proposal with an unexpected jumble of emotions. He knew at some level he was opening a Pandora's box of possibilities, both good and bad. What if he couldn't or wouldn't resist the temptation to use drugs?

Parker thought about his months behind bars. He had come to this supposedly God-forsaken prison only to find God here. What a paradox! At first Parker's compliance with the prison rules about drug use had been a mockery. He fully intended to return to using the moment he was free. Instead, he now had promises to make and commitments to keep.

Several weeks later Parker, his attorney, and Chaplain Jake met with the prison officer in charge of supervised release. The chaplain described the halfway house in Orlando and why he felt it would be a good fit. The residence had a strong reputation with drug rehabilitation and stiff requirements as to whom they accepted.

Parker affirmed his desire to complete supervised release in full compliance with the law. As he was escorted back to his cellblock, he knew God was ultimately in control. He was still getting used to this mysterious God and His strange ways. Nothing seemed impossible where God was concerned. But from Parker's angle, the future still looked foreboding. After supervised release, what? No job, no career path, no friends, and now with Gram gone, no family.

Parker's stash of faith—as small as a mustard seed—would have to see him through the time of testing. Still, he was relieved to be assigned a place with Bible study and Christ-based support groups. So much to learn. So much to lose if he gave up now. Parker's simple prayer was one Jesus loves to carry to the Father's throne: *Help me, Lord.*

Two weeks after his probationary hearing, Parker received the news that he had been mandated to the halfway house as a condition of supervised release. Chaplain Jake met with Parker routinely during the short time it took to complete the necessary paperwork for release. Drills—that's the term the chaplain assigned to these times of preparation for Parker's transfer. Chaplain Jake wanted to shore up Parker's determination to cope with difficulties through the power of the Holy Spirit.

"You're not staying clean through self-effort," Chaplain Jake repeated for the fortieth time. "You're not a better person. You're a new person, one who's forgiven of his past to walk in a new life."

Parker listened intently, wanting to understand yet admitting to himself that Jake's claims seemed preposterous. Jake opened his Bible to Romans 6:11–14 and read, "So, you too consider yourselves dead to sin, but alive to God in Christ Jesus. Therefore, do not let sin reign in your mortal body, so that you obey its desires. … For sin will not rule over you, because you are not under law but under grace."

The chaplain put down his Bible and waited for Parker's response. Parker looked past Jake's desk to an old framed print of a ship's captain steering the vessel on a stormy sea. Behind the man stood the figure of Jesus with His hand on the captain's shoulder. The chaplain turned his chair to see where Parker was staring. He admitted that the old picture was so familiar he'd forgotten it. To Parker, it hung as a silent reminder of Christ's comforting presence.

Finally Parker spoke. "I've just got to remember who's watching my back."

14

Standing outside the Orlando bus station, Parker already felt the insecurity of freedom. He had been released from prison less than two hours ago. The overcast sky threatened rain and dampened what should have been a joyful occasion. In his dreams he'd always pictured this day full of sunshine with a blue sky and fluffy clouds. Instead, the weather matched his mood. Every nerve was on edge as he waited to be picked up.

But no one was here. Not even the couple that ran the halfway house to which he'd been mandated for supervised release. Parker shuffled his feet and thought. He had the clothes on his back—the ones he had worn in to prison that cold December day almost two years ago. He had a small amount of money—his entire savings from cash he hadn't spent at the prison commissary. He could make a call inside the bus station. But whom would he call?

He had the phone number of that couple somewhere in a pocket. Connor and Megan Garrett. They obviously weren't going to show. Story of his life. Gram Sloan would say all he needed was a little stash of faith. Chaplain Jake would remind him of the one source of help available twenty-four seven. Parker had come to depend heavily on that source and had never yet received a busy signal. He was in the process of bowing his head to pray when an older Ford sedan rounded the corner and pulled up beside him.

"Hey," an African-American giant of a fellow hollered. "You Parker?"

One of the fastest answers to a prayer not yet prayed, Parker thought.

"Yeah, I'm Parker." He climbed into the car and sped away with someone he'd never met.

The two rode in silence for several minutes as the car wound through traffic and merged onto the interstate. Parker felt a cold sweat cover his body as he gripped the seat cushion. Slow down, he worried. All I need is for us to be stopped by the cops.

Once in the flow of traffic, Parker felt his heart rate slow and his breathing steady. He hadn't been in a car for almost two years. No wonder he was a little edgy. His gaze turned to his seatmate. The burly man returned his glance and spoke in a surprisingly gentle voice. "How're ya doin,' man?"

"Good," Parker lied a little.

"My name's Xander, but you can call me anything if it's dinner time." He laughed heartily at his own joke.

"I'm Parker. Parker Hamilton. But then, you knew that."

"Not too many white guys named Parker hangin' round outside a bus station." Again he laughed. Parker eased back into his seat.

"I know Mr. Connor was supposed to pick you up, but he had to go to the hospital," Xander continued. "Seems Miss Amber showed up unexpected like."

Parker's eyebrows shot up. His imagination went into full gear. Who was Miss Amber? A jilted girlfriend of a resident at the halfway house? Had a brawl broken out? Was it serious enough to send someone to the hospital?

"Sorry to hear that," Parker mumbled, fear creeping back up his spine.

Xander looked puzzled, then laughed again. "No, man, you got it wrong. Mrs. Megan—uh, Mr. Connor's wife—she birthed a baby girl this mornin'. Named her Amber Alise. I got to visit them on my way to get you. My, my, my—curly black hair, just like her ma. They goin' to have to lock that child up when she's older," Xander chuckled.

Parker felt a little foolish. "I didn't know Mrs. Megan was expecting."

"She sure wasn't expectin' three weeks early! I been up since 4 a.m. The whole place was buzzin'. Nobody was thinkin' to welcome Miss Amber yet. Her grandma won't get here 'til day after tomorrow. So, I'm kinda in charge of the place for a while. And it's my turn to cook. You goin' to have to eat my vittles this week." His laugh rumbled from deep inside.

Parker wanted to be annoyed by the man's good humor. He certainly didn't share his jovial mood. However, Xander's easy, relaxed manner had a calming effect. Maybe this new place would be halfway decent.

Parker caught himself grinning at his pun. Halfway decent. What more could a guy expect from a halfway house?

Xander took a highway exit and wound through several major intersections before turning into an older neighborhood of Orlando. Large leafy trees and well-kept lawns, newly painted exteriors and an occasional renovated home told the story of a once inner city neighborhood revitalized by new families moving into the area.

Xander pulled into the driveway of a white-shingled, two-storied house with green shutters. Parker could see a light on in an upstairs window. "We're here," Xander announced as he turned off the motor. As Parker fiddled with his seat belt, Xander loped through the light rain to the front door and unlocked it before Parker was out of the car.

"Come on in," Xander said. "We'll get you outfitted with some clothes and stuff." He took Parker through a large living and dining room, past the kitchen, and into a storage area where shelves were filled with men's clothing, sized and neatly stacked, along with toiletries, tennis shoes, and rolled socks. Parker immediately went to work finding his sizes and putting items into a cardboard box Xander provided.

"Get what you need for the next few days," he said as he headed for the kitchen. "Dinner will be ready in thirty minutes. You best be on time. It's one of the rules around here. Josh is upstairs. He's gettin' over a cold, so don't give him a hug." Xander grinned, showing perfectly white teeth. "He'll show you your space."

Parker finished filling his box, grabbing several extra containers of shampoo, deodorant, and toothpaste in case his fellow residents lived by the prison rule, *What's yours is mine, and I'll take it.* He found a back stairwell to the second floor. At the top of the steps, he stopped and took a breath. He wasn't exactly looking forward to sharing space with anyone, much less former cellies. Not that he was any better.

Chaplain Jake, who had recommended this place, was certain Parker would fit in. Applicants had to meet specific requirements: participation in church worship services and Bible study groups, therapeutic support groups, job training classes or a job, clean disciplinary record, absolutely no drug use and—most importantly—a desire for a new and different kind of lifestyle. Parker had a coveted spot, he knew. Several of his friends from the prison chapel were waiting for just such an opportunity. He had to make the most of these next six months. Slowly, he pushed open the door to the second floor—the door to his new future.

The door opened onto a long hallway. Light and music came from the front of the house, so he turned left at the first door. A slender young man sat on a twin bed between two others, strumming a guitar and singing softly. He looked up through a shock of yellow hair as Parker entered the room. He put down his guitar and stood to greet the newcomer.

"Hi, I'm Josh. You must be Parker." Parker shook his hand, then thought about the man's cold. He wiped his hand on his jeans.

"That's your bed," Josh continued, pointing at the one nearest the door. "You can put your stuff in these drawers, but hang your shirts and pants in the closet."

Josh went back to his guitar while Parker surveyed his surroundings. Although Parker had never been in the military, the room looked like he pictured an army barracks—neat but sterile: white walls, beige carpet, window blinds, and a see-through beige curtain blowing in the breeze near his bed. Each of the three beds was covered with a white cotton bedspread. The walls were bare except for a couple of framed scriptures and the serenity prayer he recognized from his prison drug recovery group.

Parker remembered the motto of Miss Louisa, the Hamilton family's housekeeper while he was growing up: everything has a place; everything in its place. After he finished putting away his toiletries, he hid the extra containers under his pillow.

He had high hopes for his stay at the halfway house, but he felt the need to proceed with caution. He knew relationships involve the vulnerability of knowing and being known. Although Parker realized he would struggle to open his heart to Josh and the others, he acknowledged a God-given mission—one Chaplain Jake had hammered into him during their drills.

"Parker, you were saved for a purpose. God has a plan for your life. Stay in step with Him, and you'll be surprised by the adventure."

The adventure had started, but without Chaplain Jake, Parker lacked confidence he could follow this unseen Presence into the unknown.

15

Parker had just finished hanging his last pair of pants when a thundering herd of men clamored up the stairwell. Josh, who had resumed his guitar solo, announced, "I thought I heard the van pull up. The guys just got home from work. They've only got fifteen minutes to clean up for dinner, so I guess we'll have introductions later."

A large older man with graying red hair lumbered into the room, grabbed a few things, and headed for the shower. He called back over his shoulder, "Hey, Parker, welcome."

"That's Harold," Josh said. "Nicest guy you'll ever want to know. But don't try to put anything over on him. Lived on the streets for years. He can flush out a lie before you tell it."

"Thanks for the warning." His heart raced. With cellies, your guard had to be up at all times. Parker would learn whether or not the guys around here could be trusted soon enough. Right now the thought of food that hadn't come from a prison kitchen lured him downstairs.

Parker followed Josh's slim form down the stairs to the dining room. A large oblong table with chairs took up most of the room. Dishes, silverware, and glasses sat on an oak sideboard along with a bucket of ice and what appeared to be pitchers of tea and milk.

Josh headed for the sideboard, so Parker followed. He sat next to Josh at the middle of the long table with a fork, knife, spoon, and a large glass of milk. On the table before him sat a huge bowl of stew, cornbread muffins, tubs of butter, and individual bowls for salad. Parker started to fill his plate, but Josh shook his head ever so slightly.

Soon the other men arrived, and after everyone was seated, Xander folded his large dark hands and bowed his head. "Lord God Almighty, thank You for this food and bless it to our bodies and our bodies to Your service." Everyone joined in the amen. Spoons and forks flew as everyone dove into the food.

"Sorry about the stew," Xander said, his mouth half stuffed with cornbread. "Mrs. Megan was goin' to the grocery store today, but you know what happened with that!" The men chuckled. "I sorta cleaned out the refrigerator."

Several mumbled their approval of the main course. "Hey, Mr. X, I've eaten worse," Harold announced, to the obvious amusement of everyone. Parker thought about Harold's life on the streets and concluded he was probably right.

The group heard a car pull into the driveway, and soon a tall, well-built man with sandy hair, glasses, and rumpled jeans came through the front door. Xander bounded to his feet. "Hey, Mr. Connor. Have a seat. I'll get what you need." He headed toward the sideboard. Everyone cheered for the new dad, who looked very tired and disheveled. Xander placed silverware and iced tea before him.

"How'd it go?" a stocky fellow across from Josh asked.

"Good, Edwin. God is good." Connor filled his bowl with stew. "Megan was in labor about seven hours, then Amber just popped out making a grand entrance and screaming at the top of her lungs. She just weighed six pounds. She and Megan are both asleep—until the first feeding."

Connor paused to take a bite. "Xander, what's in this? What do you call it?"

"It's beef stew, except for the beef." He leaned back his head and laughed. Harold joined in, and soon everyone was laughing. Parker looked from face to face. Slowly, he relaxed. A smile tugged at the corner of his lips.

Conner had briefly spoken to Parker during the meal. He apologized for not giving him a proper welcome. Parker waved away his apology. "No big deal."

Lying in bed that night, he stared at the ceiling. The window nearby was slightly open, and a soft breeze blew the beige curtain in and out. Snores came from Harold's direction, but Josh slept peacefully.

Parker couldn't sleep. Although insomnia had always been a frequent enemy, something else bothered him. Finally, it came to him. The open window and unlocked bedroom door made him feel vulnerable. Eventually, he fell asleep.

Parker awoke the next morning to the muffled sounds of his roommates quietly getting dressed. He knew they were trying not to wake him—at least not yet. He lay there thinking. An unnamed fear gripped him—not of the people around him or the neighborhood or even of his future after supervised release. Sifting through the possibilities, he identified the source: decisions.

That was it. The simplest decisions such as which pair of pants or shirts to wear or when to plant his feet on the floor brought perspiration to his brow. Parker hadn't made any decisions about his daily life for almost two years. What to wear certainly wasn't an option. Neither was getting up or going to sleep. Somebody else turned the lights on and off.

Ah, Chaplain Jake's promised adventure. What would today bring?

Parker didn't have long to wait for his answer. Harold came over to his bed and gently shook him. Parker's eyes shot open. "Sorry to wake you so early, man, but we've got pancakes waitin' on us downstairs. You come on down when you get dressed."

Harold and Josh headed to the stairwell, leaving Parker to shower and dress in privacy. As he surveyed himself in the bathroom mirror, he thought, *I need a haircut.*

If he hadn't been so hungry, Parker probably wouldn't have risked entering the dining room alone. Most of the men had finished eating and were gathering up their dishes, placing them in a large plastic container.

Xander greeted him warmly. "Parker, you done missed the hot part of the hot cakes," he grinned, pulling out a chair for the new arrival. "Sit here. Want some coffee?"

"Sure," Parker mumbled, uncomfortable with the attention. Xander brought him a steaming mug and pointed to the sugar and cream. Parker waved them away and took a sip of the brew. He choked slightly. Xander was right about his coffee-making skills.

"Help yourself to the 'cakes and syrup. Here's some sausage."

The other men waved or said hello as they filed back up the stairs. Harold squeezed Parker's shoulder as he passed. Parker wasn't sure what that was supposed to mean. The gesture was a little too friendly for his taste, but he didn't want to judge him too quickly.

"So what happens after breakfast?" Parker asked Xander.

"We got some chores to do. Then, you get to meet yo' probation officer." He stood and began placing the remainder of the dishes in the plastic tub. He carried it to the kitchen, leaving Parker alone with his thoughts.

The pancakes were cold and lumpy, the sausage hard as a rock. Still, Parker consumed the food quickly and drained his coffee cup. Xander ambled back from the kitchen carrying a pot of fresh coffee and a big, black Bible. After he refilled Parker's cup, he sat in the chair beside him.

"You missed the scripture and prayer time this mornin' before breakfast, so we'll have us a do-over," he explained matter-of-factly. This personal attention touched Parker at a deep level. He listened, nodding occasionally, amazed by this simple act of kindness. God was in this place, showing him love through another marred individual. A brother in Christ.

After breakfast cleanup, Xander and Parker climbed into the car and headed for the grocery store. Parker sat quietly, intrigued by the tree-lined boulevard and shrubs, chirping birds, and refurbished homes and businesses along the route. He relished his first daylight look at the new community he'd call home for the next few months.

When Xander pulled into a parking space at the grocery, Parker felt a moment of panic. In his privileged background, he'd only gone to a grocery store for a few items. Realizing Xander was saying something, Parker's mind snapped back to the present. Xander continued, as though Parker had heard every word of his explanation. "You push the cart. I know where stuff is."

Shopping done and groceries loaded into the trunk, the men headed back to the house. In the car Parker climbed back into his thoughts. He recalled Xander's Bible reading that morning from 2 Thessalonians 2:16–17, a passage Chaplain Jake had suggested he memorize as a life verse.

The coincidence of the reading of these verses wasn't lost on Parker. He decided to open up just a bit to Xander. He quoted: "May our Lord Jesus Christ Himself and God our Father, who has loved us and given us eternal encouragement and good hope by grace, encourage your hearts and strengthen you in every good work and word."

Zander gave him a lopsided smile. "You listen real good, man."

16

Parker sat in the crowded probation office where Xander had dropped him on his way to run errands. Men with vacant eyes sat around him, each waiting his turn. Until he'd met Malcolm, Parker had never understood how dark and hopeless his own world had become. Someone, everyone, his professors, peers, and culture had played a cruel joke on him. He had thought there was meaning in his professional achievements, but those were never enough to compensate for the lack of ultimate meaning that came only when Parker met Jesus Christ.

Still, his spiritual journey was hard. God had given him a reason to live, but Parker had to figure out the particulars. Chaplain Jake told him, "If you knew every step to take, why would you need to live by faith? Want to please God? Build your faith muscles." Time to start pumping iron, Parker concluded.

The probation officer called his name promptly at 2 p.m. and dismissed him at 2:35. In a rehearsed and mechanical rote, the officer explained the rules and consequences of violation. "And don't expect special treatment because you were a doctor," he said. "Everybody's the same with me."

Parker's eyes widened. The thought that he might consider himself a special case seemed outlandish. If anything, Parker felt more like a target than this man's superior. His time in prison had convinced him that a medical degree set him apart for persecution, not accolades.

"Yes, sir," he replied evenly.

Back in the waiting area, watching through the wall of windows for the Ford sedan to drive up, Parker debated with himself. Twelve months of this man's attitude. Could he take it? It seemed like a load until he thought about his friends in the prison chapel praying for such an opportunity. He would just have to make the most of the situation.

The days at the halfway house flew by. Megan Garrett came home with her tiny infant, followed shortly by her mother, a stout older version of her daughter with twinkling eyes and a hearty laugh. Parker liked the family immediately. He vied with the rest of the guys to hold Miss Amber, who probably hadn't slept in her crib since she arrived home.

Parker wasn't accustomed to an environment where everyone tried *not* to get on each other's nerves. Mealtimes were light-years away from eating on plastic trays surrounded by cellies. Connor insisted on common courtesies and good manners, with a lot of good-natured teasing and humor.

Parker especially liked Harold, his older roommate, who had initially made him feel uncomfortable. Harold loved people, and he didn't mind showing it. At first, Parker stiffened when Harold gave him a side hug or a playful jab. Affection had never been abundant in Hollister Hamilton's household. But Harold's physical expressions of his feelings matched his nature. Gradually, Parker realized Harold responded to everyone this way and relaxed in his presence.

He struggled to identify the reaction Harold evoked in him. One night, lying in the sanctuary of his own bed, it came to him like a thunderbolt: finally an older man appeared to accept him as he was! Parker had never measured up to Hollister's expectations. His professors—and even Dr. Andropolos—had held their distance and dangled the carrot of acceptance based on complying with their expectations.

While Chaplain Jake had nurtured him in his new faith, realistically, that was his job. Harold seemed to enjoy him for absolutely no reason at all. Parker felt the warmth of God's grace—unmerited favor—through a graying, red-haired bear of a man named Harold.

After dinner one evening, Parker mustered enough courage to ask Harold to be his sponsor in the Twelve Step program offered at the residence. While in prison, and before he became a Christian, Parker had started—and abruptly stopped—the program. When he'd read the first couple of steps of the Twelve Steps, he'd almost gasped:

Step one: We admitted we were powerless over our addiction—that our lives had become unmanageable.

The reality of his lack of control was too painful an admission for Parker at that stage of his pre-Christian world. If Parker had thought step one represented a defeat to his ego, step two loomed as a major hurdle.

Step two: came to believe that a Power greater than ourselves could restore us to sanity.

Not yet ready to accept the possibility of a higher Power, Parker had opted instead for a drug rehabilitation class. The prison's program had seemed to Parker no more effective than his school drug education classes. The "Just Say No" campaign of his elementary years had been replaced with high school images of a brain frying in a pan. Slogans abounded, but facts about drug use had done little to erase the appeal for students seeking a high or escape from their problems.

As a doctor, Parker had known the possibilities of drug interactions and overdoses; yet he had chosen to play this form of Russian roulette with his own life. Habit became dependence, which led to addiction. And nothing in his rearing and medical training had prevented the chain reaction. Now, with Harold as his sponsor, he turned to the next step.

Step three: made a decision to turn our will and our lives over to the care of God as we understood Him.

Parker's job stocking shelves in a warehouse was tiring and repetitive, but it allowed him all the time he needed to sort through his feelings, especially the ones he experienced in the support group sessions and Bible studies in the evenings at the halfway house.

Connor, who led the groups, shared bits of his life over time, and Parker pieced together a story similar to his own. The son of an upper middle class family, Connor had begun using drugs in high school. After years in and out of treatment facilities, Connor had come to know Jesus Christ as Lord and Savior. The experience turned his life around. He had dedicated his life to helping others like himself escape the trap of drug use.

Megan grew up with an alcoholic father and an enabling mother. After her mother started attending an Al Anon support group, Megan began going to a teen version of the same type group. They, along with her older sister, found Christ through loving relationships with concerned Christians in their groups.

When Megan met Connor at a group facilitator training event, she knew she had found her true love and also her calling. Together they were an impressive team, knowledgeable beyond their years about the tragedies of substance abuse, tough and confrontational when needed, but caring to the core. Parker was beginning to deposit some trust in their accounts, although he was still somewhat bewildered by their selflessness. Now he pursued step four, and it was proving to be as tough as the others.

Step Four: to make a searching and fearless moral inventory of himself.

In the support group sessions, Parker gradually unveiled the hurt and neglect of his childhood years. Tears fell; the seemingly dead spaces in Parker's heart were coming to life again.

In Hollister's tightly controlled household, no one was allowed to express anger. Now Parker's rage erupted in volcanic explosions that left him shaken and spent. Slowly, he confronted his need to forgive his father for his mental and emotional abuse.

He needed to forgive his mother for her cold indifference and obvious preference for Gavin. He even needed to forgive Alexis for taking out on him her own feelings of emotional abandonment. Gavin was the easiest to forgive. Gavin was a product of his parents' indulgence and could hardly be blamed for his self-serving ways.

What will become of Gavin? Parker wondered. At night he would lie in bed and pray for his brother, now a young adult.

Although he supposed Gavin was in Nashville, he wondered if he had finished law school. *We might as well be on different planets,* Parker thought. Somehow, some way, Parker prayed for a place in Gavin's future. First, he had to continue his own healing. Then he had to demonstrate that what God had done in his life would last—a testimony to Gram Sloan's faith and of Christ's amazing grace.

Weeks after Parker's arrival, Harold began to experience the effects of years of hard drinking. Numerous visits to the doctor and medical tests revealed he had liver disease. Treatment options were minimal. Harold was finally placed on a transplant list. Harold continued to function, although working became impossible. Rather than simply bide his time, Harold became even more intense about mentoring the young drug offenders around him.

Parker was now on step five: *admitted to God, to ourselves, and to another human being the exact nature of our wrongs.*

As difficult as he found it to share his own confessions, Parker found it more uncomfortable to hear Harold's. He realized that in his own self-centeredness, he'd not stopped to think much about helping others along on their spiritual journeys. Maybe Parker wasn't the center of this universe, after all. Bearing Harold's burdens was becoming a bountiful blessing.

Parker expected the group sessions to become easier. Surely, he'd learn how to share his feelings in this accepting environment. The process of self-scrutiny and the feelings he had suppressed about the emotional abuse he'd endured in his growing up years began to take on form and substance. His turbulent emotions were mixed with some tender memories.

Parker hadn't paused to appreciate the protection and guidance offered by Louisa, the housekeeper. He'd never thanked Clarissa, the cook, for her homespun stories that sent him into gales of laughter. Several teachers and professors had believed in his potential and poured their lives into his studies. Dr. Andropolos, for one, had invested in him a wealth of knowledge and experience to help him become the best surgeon possible.

Parker wept over the good he could have done. But he couldn't deny God's forgiveness or allow regret to overshadow the new future He had opened to him. In the past Gram Sloan had been his anchor. Now, even in death, the memory of her unyielding commitment nurtured him. The next chapter of his life would reveal step-by-step God's master plan.

17

As weeks began to turn into months, Parker began to feel like an old-timer at the halfway house. Residents came and went. Unfortunately, one of the first to go was Josh, one of his roommates. His supervised release was terminated when he was discovered with drugs in his system.

Parker had witnessed the event leading to Josh's termination. Awakened in the twilight hours of the morning by a scuffle, he peered out his bedroom window. By the light of the lamppost at the corner of the street, Parker saw someone being attacked by three men. Parker jumped out of bed and quickly donned the jeans he'd left lying across a wooden chair in the corner. His eyes darted to Josh's empty bed. Harold slept on, unaware of the incident happening below.

As he rushed downstairs, Parker heard the screech of car tires on pavement. He flung open the front door and rushed to where Josh lay on the grass. Parker's medical instincts took over as he checked Josh's pulse and assessed his wounds.

Connor came flying out of the house buttoning his shirt with one hand while dialing 9-1-1.

"Give me your shirt," Parker hollered. Connor threw his shirt toward Parker, who quickly used it to stanch the bleeding from a wound in Josh's shoulder. Connor looked quizzically at Parker, who explained, "Josh's been stabbed. Let's move him under the lamppost where I can get a better look."

The two men easily lifted Josh's slight frame. As Parker worked to stop the bleeding, Connor talked to the 9-1-1 operator. Soon Megan arrived on the scene and looked with horror at Josh's bloody clothing. As the EMT's arrived, the whole household poured from the front door.

"Let's pray," Harold shouted, and the men gathered in a huddle. The medical team loaded Josh into the ambulance. Connor hopped in the front seat. Parker watched with muddled thoughts. His concern for Josh gave way to fear. *I'm not supposed to practice medicine,* he reminded himself. *Did I do anything wrong? Am I going to be arrested?*

Back inside, the somber residents gathered around the dining table—some praying, others singing softly, and a few lost in memories of their own brushes with death. Megan brewed coffee, and they waited in silence for Connor's phone call.

Around 4 o'clock Connor called Megan. After hearing his report, she held the phone to her chest as she relayed to the men that Josh was out of surgery. However, drugs had shown up in his blood work. When he recovered, Josh would be taken back to prison.

"But what happened?" Harold asked.

"A drug buy gone bad." Megan was almost whispering, shaken by the thought of what had been going on right under their noses. "The police were able to get a statement from Josh before he went into surgery." Megan paused, aware that Connor had asked her a question.

Megan handed the phone to a stunned Parker. "He wants to talk to you."

"H-hello," he stammered. "Did I do something wrong?"

"Only helped save a man's life, that's all. I wanted to thank you. I'm proud of you, Parker. I wouldn't have known what to do."

Parker breathed an audible sigh of relief. "Thank God. Thank God," he repeated, meaning every word.

When Josh had recovered enough to have visitors, he asked the guard outside his door if he could see Parker. "Come on," he begged. "I've got to thank the guy who saved my life." The officer in charge gave permission for the visit.

Parker didn't like the ride to the hospital in a police car or the police escort to Josh's room. In fact, he didn't like the idea of entering a hospital. Parker thought back to his frequent visits to hospital morgues while he served in the medical examiner's office. Not a pleasant experience, he concluded. At the time, such trips had all been part of the job, and the bodies were meaningless people in a meaningless world.

Entering Josh's room, Parker was surprised to see the young man sitting up in bed, a breakfast tray before him. Josh was struggling to butter his toast, his left arm and shoulder swathed in bandaging. Parker finished the task for him, grateful for something to do to postpone an awkward conversation.

As Parker applied jelly to the toast, Josh began expressing his gratitude and apologizing for the behavior that had cost him his chance for release. Parker didn't know what to say. Although Josh was using the appropriate words, Parker sensed his remarks were rehearsed. Something was missing. After Josh's lengthy explanation of why and how he'd begun to use drugs again, Parker said his goodbyes and wished Josh well, saying for all the residents how much he would be missed.

On the ride back to the halfway house, Parker had an aha moment. Excuses. Explanations. Reasons. Some blaming. Some self-loathing. Josh had reacted like most addicts, caught in the emotional traps of what his support group called stinkin' thinkin'. Parker recalled his own battles with drugs and his resolve to pursue a new way of life. *Why am I one of the lucky ones?* he asked himself. The only answer was grace.

Connor remained shaken that drugs had been bought outside his house and used right under his roof. Not only did the reputation of the halfway house suffer but also his personal sense of worth. He and Megan thought they were instilling the right values and insisting on the strictest behaviors in their therapy regimen. What had gone wrong?

One night after the group session, Parker stayed behind with Connor. The two men sat on floor pillows, legs crossed, avoiding each other's eyes.

Parker felt Connor's confusion and wounded spirit. He wasn't sure he had any words of comfort, but finally he broke the silence. "Everybody's got to come to it himself." Immediately Parker realized his words came out of the blue.

"What I mean is, you can't make the decision to stay clean for other people. No matter how good your instruction or modeling, people make their own choices." Connor sat, immobile.

Parker continued, "That's how God set it up. He gave us free choice. Josh chose his own path. You're not responsible."

Connor took in Parker's words. Then he sighed. "Thanks for saying that, Parker. I guess I needed some reassurance. I try so hard—"

"But you have to leave the results with God," Parker concluded. "You know, Josh's story isn't over. At one point in my life, my Gram Sloan might easily have given up on me. But she kept writing me until she grew so feeble she couldn't write anymore. God had a plan for me, and He has a plan for Josh."

18

The police made residents of the halfway house aware of continuing drug activity in their neighborhood. Both as a warning and a challenge, Parker's probation officer came around frequently, often performing a pat down and search of his bedroom. Parker was clean—to the man's disappointment. But the officer's suspicions remained, especially since Parker had been the first on the scene when Josh was stabbed.

Parker lay awake at night. Occasionally, he heard the voices of people walking down the street, and the lamppost still allowed enough light to see if any illegal activity was occurring. He placed a notepad and pencil on the bedside table in case he had information for the police.

On a couple of occasions, groupings of men appeared suspicious, but whatever they were doing happened quickly, and they disappeared into the darkness. Not enough time or details offered him the chance to alert the authorities.

Often Parker found himself on his knees by the window, not knowing exactly who or what he was praying for but unable to stop thinking about the hurting people who thought drugs were the answer. One night as Parker kneeled beside his bed, Harold woke himself with a loud snort and opened his eyes. His head turned toward the only source of light in the room—the lamppost outside the open window.

When Harold glimpsed the silhouette of Parker's form, his first thought was that Parker was sick. He threw off his sheet and sat up. "You ok?" Harold asked.

The sudden question startled Parker. "Yeah. Just praying."

"All right, I'll join you. What are we prayin' about?"

Parker thought for a moment. Harold wasn't going to buy in to any half-truth he might tell him. At the same time, he didn't want to worry anyone about drug activity if nothing was, in fact, going on. "I was praying about Josh," Parker whispered convincingly.

"I'm with you, brother." Harold joined Parker on his knees beside the bed. With shoulders almost touching, the two interceded for their former roommate, now asleep in a jail cell awaiting transport back to prison.

Parker slept fitfully. Ninety minutes later, the sound of a car stopping in front of the house pulled him out of a bad dream. He looked out the window and saw a silver convertible idling at the curb. Two men approached it cautiously and handed something to the driver. Parker got a clear view of the driver. He reached for his pencil, then stared in disbelief.

The profile of the man was a younger version of his father, Hollister Hamilton. There was no mistaking it. Parker had just witnessed his brother Gavin making a drug deal right in front of the halfway house. The silver car streaked off into the dark.

Parker dropped to his knees and prayed that if he had indeed seen Gavin buying drugs, his brother would come back to the neighborhood, back to the curb, back to a place where he could intercept him. He planned what he would say, rehearsing Gavin's possible comebacks to his arguments and how he'd answer them.

Parker was willing to beg. Willing to do whatever it took to spare his brother the inevitable fate of being caught with drugs. Or worse, getting seriously hurt like Josh. At least Gavin could pay for his drugs. He wasn't likely to be killed.

But after a few nights, Gavin hadn't returned. Parker fretted as he dreamed of silver sedans, knife fights, blood, and sirens. On Saturday, during a brief excursion in the van with Connor to pick up supplies at a hardware store, Connor asked him, "Something bothering you?"

"No," Parker answered, a little too quickly. "Just tired." He couldn't tell Connor about seeing Gavin or his suspicions that drugs were still sold outside their house. Connor would undoubtedly tell the police. Parker couldn't take that chance, not while Gavin was possibly still in town.

In church Sunday morning Parker sat on the row with the other residents listening absentmindedly to the message. His thoughts returned to Gavin and the puzzle his life presented. What would have led Gavin to use drugs? None of the reasons (or excuses) for Parker's drug abuse seemed to fit.

Gavin had his parents' attention and indulgence. He had his father's blessing in his vocation and probably a job in the Hamilton law firm. Gavin had an education, money, friends. He'd always seemed in control, if not more than a little controlling. What did drugs offer?

Maybe escape from the boredom of too much? Parker wondered. He brushed aside the thought. Recreational drug users didn't need to go alone to a street corner in a strange town. The puzzle pieces weren't fitting together.

Sunday night he fell asleep from exhaustion almost the moment his head hit the pillow. He didn't awaken until the morning light filtered through his open window. His eyes flickered open. Parker got up and kneeled beside his bed, seeking protection for a brother he barely knew.

Parker waited until he was sure his father's law offices were open on Monday morning. With unsteady hands he dialed the familiar number, having gained permission from his boss for the long distance call.

"Sure, it's nothing," Omir offered. He had waved away the bills Parker extended. "Use my office."

On the second ring an unfamiliar, perky young voice answered. "May I speak to Gavin Hamilton?" Parker asked.

"I'm sorry, but Mr. Hamilton isn't available today," the voice replied. "May I transfer you to his voice mail?"

Thinking quickly, Parker responded, "Let me talk to my father, to—er, to—Hollister Hamilton."

A brief silence, followed by a crisp "Thank you," and his call was transferred to Ruby, Hollister's longtime secretary. Her voice brought back pleasant memories. "Ruby, it's Parker, Parker Hamilton." He waited for her intake of breath, then continued. "Ruby, I'm trying to contact Gavin. Can you put me through to him?"

Ruby, obviously flustered, seemed unwilling to simply give him an answer. "Why, Parker, how are you? Where are you?" she asked, sympathy in her tone.

Knowing he needed to acknowledge her questions, Parker gave her a quick review of his whereabouts and asked about her family and health.

Then he returned to the reason for his call. "Ruby, I think I saw Gavin here in Orlando this past weekend. Is that possible?"

"Well, yes, as a matter of fact, it is. He's vacationing there with some friends from law school. My, isn't that a coincidence! Did he see you?"

"No—no, I don't think so," Parker stammered. "How can I reach him?"

Ruby hesitated, caught between competing loyalties. "It's a private number, Parker," she replied. "I'm not at liberty to give it out."

Parker took in the implications. "Okay. Is he—is Gavin all right? I mean, as far as you know?"

Ruby fumbled for words. "Well, yes, as far as I know. I really don't see him much. My work keeps me so busy ..." Her words trailed off.

Sensing that further probing would get him nowhere, Parker thanked her and said goodbye. He leaned against the office wall, eyes shut tightly. *Gavin was in that car I saw. I'm sure of it. And he's somewhere close by, close enough to choose a drug pickup point right outside my bedroom window. How will I ever find him?*

Omir came back to his office. "You ok, Parker? You look bad."

Parker quickly composed himself. "Everything's fine," he lied, not too convincingly. "He wasn't there. I'll try again when I get home." Parker headed back to the warehouse, back to his thoughts as he stacked shelves in the sweltering humidity.

Why had God burdened him with sighting Gavin outside his window? What could he do about his brother's situation? A sudden—and Parker's first—urge to escape to the fog of a drug-induced nothingness enveloped him. Reality was simply too tough. Parker had precedent for giving up, for taking a detour on the narrow road Jesus described in Matthew 7:13–14.

Harold had taken many detours. Parker recalled another of the residents who had slipped back into drug use when life became overwhelming. Fortunately, Parker recognized his stinkin' thinkin' before he acted on it. Chaplain Jake's voice thundered in his ears: "Try to solve a problem, not make it worse! Only cowards turn back."

Parker gave his despair to the only One who had given His all to the Father's care.

19

During one of the evening Bible study classes, an unexpected visitor rang the doorbell and asked for Parker. Connor escorted him into the living room filled with men sitting on every available surface, Bibles open in their laps.

"Parker, why don't you take your guest to the kitchen table," Connor suggested.

As the two men headed to the kitchen, Parker glanced out the window to see a red Ferrari in the driveway. The stranger looked wealthy enough to be the driver. Dressed in his standard discount store jeans and a tee shirt, Parker was certainly curious about the man but not intimidated. He was learning not to judge too quickly by outward appearances.

The two men sat across from each other at the table. "Care for some coffee?" Parker volunteered.

"No, thanks," he replied. The man gathered some papers from a briefcase before placing it on the floor at his feet. "I'm attorney Matthew Brocking from the Orlando firm of Salter, Gibbons, and Sterns." He positioned a hand across the table, and the men shook.

"Obviously, you know who I am," Parker grinned. "What can I do for you?"

"I believe I have some important information for you," Brocking announced. He talked for the next few minutes, then extended papers for Parker to examine. As he continued, Parker's eyes grew wide, his head shaking slightly in disbelief.

Finally, Brocking concluded, "As soon as you have your—ah—legal affairs in order, we'll be in touch. Until then, here is my card."

Parker accepted the card and stood as Brocking returned the papers to his briefcase, turned toward the living room door, and disappeared into the night. Parker shut the front door and quietly returned to the seat he had vacated in the living room.

When the Bible study concluded, everyone left for upstairs except for Parker and Connor. Connor raised an eyebrow and waited to hear the identity of the stranger.

Parker knew Connor had earned the right to know the reason for this mysterious man's visit. But the news was too overwhelming, too unsettling—yet humbling. Too amazing for words. After a lengthy pause, he explained. "The man is a lawyer from a firm here in Orlando. My father's law office contacted him to deliver some information to me."

Parker hadn't told Connor about his call to his father's office the previous week. Although he'd never considered his whereabouts a mystery to anyone who wanted to find him, knowing his father had his present address probably accounted for the attorney's visit.

"Are you in any trouble?" Connor asked with heartfelt concern.

"No, no trouble. Just—well, this news is a game-changer."

Parker began his story in a soft tone as though telling a secret. "You know, Connor," he began, "my father and I aren't exactly on good terms." Connor nodded, well aware of the tension in the father-son relationship.

"It seems Father is finally getting around to telling me something I should probably have known a year ago when my grandmother's will was read. He was displeased with the way Gram Sloan chose to dispose of her home in Kentucky and the horse farm her family had owned for three generations."

Parker took a deep breath. He pictured his father's face tensing, teeth clenched as his cheeks grew redder, eyebrows turning inward, a scowl replacing what must have been a serene smile as he awaited what he thought would be news of his good fortune.

"According to the documents faxed to this local law firm, Gram Sloan left the majority of her estate to me." He watched Connor's jaw drop. He continued, "That is, provided I complete my sentence successfully and prove to have been rehabilitated."

Connor whistled beneath his breath. "What kind of money are we talking about?"

"Eight figures, maybe more. Obviously, her estate hasn't been settled. Hollister is fighting the will, claiming Gram was psychologically unfit when she signed the revised document shortly after I went to prison. Mr. Brocking, the local attorney, seems to think Hamilton's got a strong case. Proving I'm rehabilitated would be a matter for the court to interpret. My father knows every judge in Davidson County, where the will was filed."

Connor sat still, waiting for the rest of Parker's thoughts.

"I don't deserve Gram's money. Part of me wants to just give in, let my father have it, forget trying to win against him. Another part of me wants to prove that Gram's trust wasn't in vain. She obviously believed in me, in my future. I don't want to let her down."

Parker's voice began to tremble and tears inched their way down his cheeks. "Gram loved me—loved me for my sake and not what I could do for her. She was always there when I needed her. She sat in a courtroom and heard me sentenced for my crimes, yet she willed me her estate. It makes no sense!"

When Parker didn't continue, Connor spoke softly. "Kind of like Christ dying for us while we were still sinners."

Parker sniffed and nodded.

"She must have loved you very much."

20

Parker's first six months in the halfway house approached. He had six months to go in his year of supervised release. Connor and Megan would make the decision as to whether or not he could continue in their program. Would his location change? Where would he go? He knew the time for their decision was still days away, but the idea of having to transfer from their loving care was too frightening to dismiss casually.

The following day Parker caught Connor sitting alone at the kitchen table staring at a stack of papers. Maybe now would be a good time to talk. He caught Connor's attention and asked, "If you have a minute, may I say something to you?"

He motioned for Parker to take a seat across from him.

"I don't know what I would have done without you and Megan these past few months. You've been such a—"

"Hey, man. Don't go saying goodbyes," Connor interrupted. "You're going to be seeing me around for a while longer. That is, if you want." Parker stared at him, head cocked to one side, wondering if this was the good news he'd been hoping for.

"Megan and I have been thinking. You remember Xander, right?"

He grinned. As though anyone could forget Xander. Parker had watched with great pride when Xander graduated from the program and went home to the city of East St. Louis to work in a youth mentoring program. The nonprofit organization would benefit from Xander's enthusiasm, jovial disposition, and fundraising ability. He felt sure when Xander recounted his own story, no one in the audience would leave with dry eyes.

Now he responded to Connor's question with a fond memory. "Six months ago, on my first day at the halfway house, Xander read me a Scripture. Just happened to be a Scripture I'd taken as my life verse from 2 Thessalonians 2:16–17: 'May our Lord Jesus Christ Himself and God our Father, who has loved us and given us eternal encouragement and good hope by grace, encourage your hearts and strengthen you in every good work and word.' I'll never forget Xander, and the 'coincidence' of those words. Why do you ask?" Parker inquired.

Connor continued, "We'd like you to stay on at the halfway house in a role similar to the one Xander played. When your next six months of supervision are up, then you can think about next steps. Remember, we've got to get you rehabilitated." He grinned.

Parker jumped at the chance. Decision made, he moved into Xander's first floor bedroom near the kitchen, sleeping in a room by himself for the first time since his incarceration. Although he enjoyed his privacy, the windows of the room faced the small backyard. No longer could he watch and pray facing the streetlight out front—hoping yet despairing to see Gavin again.

The halfway house residents gathered on the front lawn when the ambulance came to transport Harold to his mother's home in Alabama. Awaiting a liver transplant he knew would probably never happen, Harold had one last word for the friends he was leaving behind.

"Guys, God loves you. Don't ever forget that." Harold paused for breath, then pointed to his gurney. "Hard drinking and hard living has left me like this. Don't go back to that life. Here's where you'll end up."

Each person passed by to receive a bear hug from the man who'd been a father figure or big brother to all of them. Parker waited until the end of the line. "Harold, you're a sign of God's grace in my life. You loved me for no reason. You showed me God's unconditional love. I'll never forget you."

Harold leaned over to speak softly into Parker's ear. "I once dreamed of opening my own halfway house. But my demons never seemed to let go long enough for that to happen. Parker, pray about it. It would mean the world to me."

Parker straightened to watch as Harold was loaded into the ambulance. *What was that supposed to mean?* he wondered. *Did Harold know he might come into some money?* He felt certain Connor hadn't betrayed his secret inheritance. Parker turned back toward the house to find Connor staring intently in his direction. Had Connor overheard the conversation? What did he make of Harold's request?

Parker felt a familiar warmth creep up his neck. Surely, Connor had seen tears filling his eyes. When would he ever grow accustomed to having his feelings exposed? Maybe, just maybe, that was all right.

Parker's progress on the Twelve Steps of AA halted with the absence of Harold. Gradually, Harold's role shifted to another man named Edwin. Parker had met Edwin on his first night at the halfway house. He'd appeared to be a silent type without much to add to the lively discussions around their Bible studies or support groups.

Edwin had been accused of money laundering, to which he'd pleaded innocent. In prison, and through the influence of an unofficial cellmate Bible study, he'd become a Christian. Now serving his own supervised release, he faced not only the rigors of parole but a hefty fine for his misdeeds.

Parker soon learned the adage: *quiet streams run deep.* Like Harold, Edwin was savvy to the misleading statements, excuses, or blaming common to the residents. Unlike Harold, he wasn't physically demonstrative of his affection. However, his penetrating brown eyes invited honesty and commitment. Follow through was Edwin's motto. He agreed to take over Harold's sponsorship of several of the men if they worked the twelve steps with the intensity of a match lighting the end of a stick of dynamite. Parker took up step six: *were entirely ready to have God remove all these defects of character.*

The guys worked with the memory of Harold fresh in their minds. Three months later, Harold passed away quietly in his sleep.

21

Parker enjoyed his new responsibilities in the role Zander had once played. The first time he drove to the federal prison where he had been incarcerated to pick up a new resident for the halfway house, he'd stopped in to see Chaplain Jake.

With deep emotion, he shared the news of Gram Sloan's will and the burden he now carried to see the process of rehabilitation through. The two men might have talked forever if a guard hadn't come by to say, "Hey, Chaplain, you got an appointment out here asking your whereabouts."

During the day Parker oriented new residents, helped with paperwork, provided transportation, supervised chores, and even learned to cook a decent meal. In the evenings Connor and he led the support group meetings. Connor had also enrolled Parker in Bible correspondence courses, hoping he'd soon be able to lead the weekly Bible studies on his own.

Although Parker's days were more than full, he slept fitfully. Sometimes, he'd awaken and wander into the living room, where he would assume his post looking out the front window. Deep within him he felt God had planted a longing to make a difference in his brother's life. Only God could make that happen. Parker's repeated calls to his father's office had brought no response from Gavin. Had Ruby told Gavin Parker had seen him in Orlando? If so, was he afraid Parker would alert Hollister to the drug buy? Or had he even connected the two events?

Months later, Parker stood in front of a judge to hear the welcomed words that his supervised release had ended. He had paid his debt to society in full and was now free to pursue his future. For one, he could apply to have his medical license reinstated. He reasoned, *I don't have the means to set up a practice. No one is going to hire me to work in their practice with my background. … My surgical skills are rusty. … It just wouldn't work.*

Without medicine, what other skills did he have? A new career path would require funds. The chief fly in the ointment continued to be Parker's father—and Hollister's determination to get his hands on Gram Sloan's inheritance. As long as Parker stayed clear of drug use, Hollister's claim on the money was doubtful. Parker felt strongly that if he had any chance of redemption, it would need to be in Nashville, under his father's watchful gaze but certainly without his blessing.

He also wanted to be near Gavin should God open the door to a relationship with him. Waiting … definitely his least favorite part of the Christian life.

Parker and Connor spent long hours discussing his next steps. A nonprofit organization seemed the most likely to employ him. Connor called them "redemption centers." He said they helped people trade the bad in their lives for good. Parker liked that description.

Although Connor contacted several nonprofits in the Nashville area, a position for Parker hadn't opened as yet. One day Connor got a call from a Dr. Ted Poole. He volunteered at a nonprofit medical clinic in Nashville located near two large hospitals off Charlotte Boulevard. Dr. Poole had gone through Vanderbilt Medical School with Parker. Through Connor's repeated contacts with mutual friends, he had heard of his situation.

When Connor hung up the phone, he found Parker at the kitchen table helping a new resident fill out some paperwork. Connor asked Megan to take over and waved Parker toward the living room to talk. An hour's discussion and prayer time ended with a hug and the familiar tears Parker had now come to welcome during special times with the Lord.

In a matter of days, Parker boarded a plane to Nashville and spent a long weekend with Ted Poole; his wife, Susan; their two children; and a large Lab named Theodore. "Susie said the dog is a chip off the old block," Ted grinned. "Polite, good with children, and a mess to clean up after. So she named him Theodore."

The Pooles lived in the Woodmont area, a short distance from the campus where Parker had first met Ted. Somehow news that Dr. Poole was on the board of medical licensure for the state of Tennessee came as no surprise to Parker. Always amazed at God's provision, he sensed His hand in this reunion of two men whose lives had taken very different paths.

After a noisy informal dinner around the Pooles' dining table, the guys headed for Ted's study while Susan got the children ready for bed. Coffee cups in hand, Parker felt at ease talking to Ted about his past. He felt comfortable enough to share his pending legal battle with his father over Gram Sloan's will. He needed a means of proving he had not only paid his debt to society but also was a reputable member of the community. Ted sat silently, already aware of the information Connor had shared confidentially.

Parker knew Ted and Connor had talked about a nonprofit medical clinic, but he had no idea what role he might play.

"What about returning to medicine?" Ted asked. "I can help you get your license to practice here in Tennessee."

Parker let the thought sink in. He'd resigned himself never to practice medicine again. The idea that he might not have to give it up simply wouldn't compute. His stash of faith was waning. "I don't see that happening."

Ted started to reply when two pajama-clad children hopped in his lap for goodnight kisses.

22

On Saturday Ted and Parker toured the clinic with Theodore padding silently alongside. The converted house worked well as a medical facility, and every nook and cranny was spotlessly clean. With the golden Lab sleeping comfortably between them, the two men poured over records of client services, volunteer and paid staff, donors, and debts. Parker recognized several of the donor names as friends of his family.

On Sunday Parker rode with the Poole family to church. Sitting in the front seat of their SUV, he wondered what this church would be like. The church the residents attended in Orlando was filled with friendly and accepting members, but the men always felt conspicuous. This Sunday, Parker was just a friend of a friend. Would he see anyone from his former life? Would they know his present circumstances?

"Our church is very casual," Ted had told him. "No one wears a suit except our pastor, Frank Norwell, and I think he does it out of habit."

The SUV pulled up in front of a traditional brick building with a steeple that seemed to reach to heaven. Inside, several people greeted them, including a fortyish couple with their young adult daughter. Ted introduced him. "I'd like you to meet Layton and Amy Brooks and their daughter, Brianne."

Parker extended his hand, which Layton gripped with a firm handshake. After the families were seated, Ted whispered, "Layton is my mentor. We meet every Tuesday for breakfast."

As the service began, Parker's attention was drawn to the only man in a suit, sitting on stage with his legs crossed, beaming as an ensemble led a familiar praise song. *He's got the kindest eyes,* Parker thought. *Pastor Frank reminds me of someone.* His mind darted to the face of his own mentor and friend, Chaplain Jake. Memories rushed in of Malcolm, Xander, Harold, Connor and Megan—a long list of names of those who had been wounded by life and yet had left him their legacies of faith.

Early Monday morning Ted and Parker arrived at the clinic before it opened. Ted introduced him to Kathy Collins, the receptionist and bookkeeper. "Her husband is a local pastor who's been very supportive of our ministry." Ted left him there to get acquainted while he made rounds at nearby Centennial Hospital.

When Ted returned, Parker was sitting in the waiting room with a baby on one knee and a toddler playing at his feet. "Their mom is seeing the doctor," Parker explained. "I think all the months of rocking Amber have paid off."

"Apparently," Ted observed. "But I've got to get you to the airport." Out of a dimly lit corner appeared a young girl, probably an older sibling, who took charge of the children while Parker collected his jacket. As they drove away, Ted suggested they stop for breakfast at a hotel near the airport terminal.

Over coffee and bagels Ted announced as matter-of-factly as he could, "You know we need a medical director at the clinic. You'd have the honor of being the lowest paid doctor in the county. Susie and I have a guesthouse over our garage that's been empty since Susie's mom died of cancer two years ago. You could live there. We could make this work."

When Parker didn't respond, Ted added, "I know you have a calling on your life. This job wouldn't have to last forever. Think of it as a means to an end."

Parker furrowed his brow while the idea germinated. The words of Psalm 37:4 popped into his mind, a scripture Megan had embroidered and hung near the front door of their house in Orlando: "Take delight in the Lord, and He will give you your heart's desires."

The airplane touched down on the tarmac at Nashville International Airport. He'd said very tearful goodbyes to Megan, Conner, little Amber, and the men at the halfway house. Ted picked him up and drove him to the garage apartment that would serve as his home for the indefinite future.

"I found you a car," Ted announced as they pulled in front of the garage. Parker's eyebrows shot up. "I know, I know. I went out on a limb here, but you don't have time to shop for one. Tomorrow we've got to get you your driver's license. We needed you at the clinic yesterday."

With his medical license still awaiting approval by the state board, Parker began work at the clinic in an administrative role only. After his licensure came through, he began seeing and referring patients to the other volunteer staff, including Ted. Parker's medical training had been thorough, but he had to brush up on his treatment of everyday ailments, pediatrics, and maternity care.

His heart broke to think that his patients would have been turned away by other doctors or facilities due to their lack of money or insurance. Most were just scraping by without large medical bills. Every day he awoke with gratitude that God had given him an education and a skill set worthy of the task.

He also had the freedom to share Christ's message of hope for an eternal dwelling without sorrow or tears. Those who became believers took the gospel of salvation home to dozens of family and friends. Parker was truly able to say to them, "There but for the grace of God, go I."

23

Parker leaned back in the cracked leather office chair behind his ancient oak desk. He planted his feet on the recently cleared-off surface, pencil to his lips. He'd thought very little about what he would say to his colleagues at his going-away party. How could he ever put his feelings into words? How could he tell the staff and volunteers at the medical clinic goodbye?

He stared absentmindedly out his one window to the left of the open door. Three years. He couldn't believe it. In some ways the years had passed quickly. In other ways, time had crawled at a snail's pace. He rarely allowed himself the luxury of sitting still and contemplating life, but today was different—in fact, exceptional. Today marked a turning point—the end of one era and the beginning of another.

When Ted Poole had proposed the idea of Parker becoming the clinic's medical director, he'd acknowledged Parker had another calling on his life. Thanks to Gram Sloan and her inheritance, he would now be able to open a halfway house in the spring. Harold's dream—as well as Parker's—would actually come true!

Still amazed at God's hand so evident in the circumstances, Parker recalled Hollister on one side of the courtroom and him on the other. The scene had formerly been his ultimate nightmare. Hollister hadn't been accustomed to losing—especially where a great amount of money was concerned. Proving he had been rehabilitated had been very easy. Witnesses lined up practically out the courthouse door.

The tougher part had been backing away from his father's offer to end the lawsuit by settling for half, then a third of Gram's fortune. The old Parker would have let Hollister have his way, if for no other reason than to gain some favor in his father's eyes. The new Parker determined that Gram Sloan's money should go to a third party—not in either of their pockets.

A new halfway house for recovering addicts, most of whom would come directly from a prison cell, appropriately suited the purpose for which Gram had left Parker her estate. Enough money would be left to fund The Sloan Foundation, which would keep the doors open. Parker felt her presence throughout the court hearing and almost heard a shout from heaven when the verdict was announced.

The one dark spot was his lack of contact with Gavin, who'd never returned his calls or shown up for any of the court proceedings. The brothers might as well have been a continent away from each other instead of a matter of miles.

"Come on," Ted hollered from the hallway. "Let's get this party rolling!"

He rose to his feet and joined his colleagues in the waiting room, which the receptionist, Kathy, had made festive with banners and balloons. In the receiving line, he shook the hands of well-wishers, including the clinic's board members and prominent donors.

Among them stood Layton Brooks, Parker's mentor and friend. Layton had a long history of mentoring men in Pastor Frank's church, including Ted Poole. Layton shook his hand. "Hey, Parker, come by the house on your way home. Amy and I would like that very much."

"Sure," Parker agreed, surprised by the offer. The Brooks and Pooles lived close by but had never socialized. He knew Layton's wife Amy only to say hello.

The crowd hushed as Kathy's husband, Rev. Roy Collins, led the prayer for the meal. After a buffet of cold cuts, veggies, fruits, and dips, Kathy cut the cake bearing the simple words, "Thank You." Then Ted introduced the program for the part Parker was dreading. He wished he could vanish into thin air. Accolades made him feel uncomfortable— probably due to their rare usage in his growing up years. Parker sighed as Ted launched into his speech. While the clinic had grown in its endowment and services under Parker's leadership, Ted would surely have to acknowledge God's fingerprints in all that had been accomplished.

Later, Parker would have trouble recalling what he said in response to the glowing comments. He knew his words had come from the heart. As much as he regretted leaving these dear friends, the time had come for his new ministry.

The evening ended with a benediction from Pastor Frank Norwell, Parker's pastor now. "Father," Pastor Frank concluded, "we commend to You The Sloan House in East Nashville. May its doors ever be open to those whom You are in the process of redeeming for Your name's sake. Amen."

"Amen," Parker whispered, "So be it, Lord."

Parker and Layton arrived at his house at the same time. Amy invited Parker to take a seat on the couch. A petite redhead, she radiated joy, especially when she glanced her husband's way. The connection between them seemed to flow effortlessly. He looked at his feet, almost embarrassed to witness such intimacy.

Amy left for the kitchen to get coffee. Just then a similarly petite strawberry blonde appeared around the corner, headed for the front door. "Bye, Dad," she waved—then stopped. "Oh, I didn't know you had company."

Parker stood for the introductions.

"Parker, my daughter Brianne. This is Dr. Parker Hamilton."

"I've seen you around church," said Brianne as she looked up at him with sparkling blue eyes. "You're hard to miss."

Parker blushed at the reference to his height. He shook her delicate hand. Her dad explained the men's friendship, and Brianne hurried on out the door. It was then that Parker noticed her prosthesis.

"She's twenty-two, getting her MBA at Belmont," Layton beamed, referring to another university in Nashville. He didn't mention her disability, so Parker didn't either.

When Amy returned, they sipped coffee while Parker answered her questions about his past and present. He'd had enough experience giving his backstory—what believers called his testimony—that the words about his life before receiving Christ were out before he even considered the embarrassing parts of the narrative.

"I'm guessing you two have a testimony of your own," he ventured. The couple openly shared their own story of tragedy and triumph, giving God the glory for their restored marriage and Brianne's recovery from childhood cancer. That accounted for her prosthesis, he surmised.

When Parker discovered that Amy was an interior decorator, he perked up. "Do I have an offer for you! Of course, it's an unpaid volunteer position." They laughed, all having much experience with such *opportunities*. Parker explained that he would soon be opening a rehabilitation halfway house in East Nashville. He needed some serious help with furnishing and decorating the place.

Amy graciously offered to help, ideas already beginning to bubble to the surface. Then Layton stood and motioned for them to follow him. "Come, I want to show you something."

He led them to a room down a long hallway to his man cave. A *Keep Out* sign on the door had been marked with a red X and childish handwriting, *Come on In*. Parker laughed.

"I want to show you my trophy case." Layton moved the three of them toward a large cabinet at the end of the room. He explained the idea of presenting a trophy to his spiritual mentors, who had displayed character traits he wanted to develop in his life.

He proudly took out four of the trophies and described why he'd selected each person. Parker easily understood how Amy had shown *forgiveness* and Brianne, *endurance*. Hearing the stories of Myra Norwell's *peace* in her suffering and Meme Dyer's *hope* blessed him.

From another shelf, Layton produced two more trophies. "Parker, I want to present a trophy to Gram Sloan *in absentia*—but present with the Lord. The trophy is for *faith*. I don't know of a story more representative of that characteristic. Her family inheritance was her 'little stash of faith,' a down payment on all that God had in store for you. She had faith in you, but, ultimately, her faith was in God, who had already been doing His work of grace in your life."

Parker accepted the trophy with tear-filled eyes.

"But I also have one for you, Parker." Layton placed the second trophy in his friend's other hand. "It's the *freedom* award. You are free in Christ. Free from the slavery of sin to serve the Savior."

Now Layton and Amy teared up as well.

"If you don't mind, I'll keep them here in my trophy case of grace," Layton said, arranging the trophies back on their shelves. "They remind me of qualities I want the Holy Spirit to develop in my life." He turned to Parker and put a hand on his shoulder.

"Tonight marks a significant transition in your life. Our mentoring relationship is coming to an end. You've got several men you'll soon be mentoring at the halfway house, and I've got a fellow who wants to meet with me. That's how God intends His kingdom of disciples to grow."

The three held hands while Layton prayed a prayer of blessing over his friend. When Parker pulled away from the house, his thoughts turned to portions of Galatians 5:1–2, 14: *It is for freedom that Christ has set us free. Stand firm, then ... serve one another in love.*

Soon he'd be able to help men stand firm in their freedom from the slavery of sin. He was free ... to serve.

25

Parker stood on the front porch of the Sloan House talking with the general contractor. Nearby a painter retouched the white columns framing the wrap-around porch, which would eventually contain a swing and numerous wrought iron chairs and tables.

A small square-cut car turned into the gravel driveway. A pert strawberry blonde climbed out, waving to Parker. "Dad and Mom asked me to bring you this." She lifted a large package from the passenger seat and walked toward the men. "A housewarming gift," she explained.

Parker hurried to take the bundle from her. "Thanks, Brianne. How are your parents? I missed my appointment with Amy yesterday."

Brianne squeezed her small frame past the painter and onto the porch. "I know. Why do you think I'm delivering this package?" She extended her hand to the contractor.

Parker made the introductions. "This is Peter Riggs. Peter, this is Brianne Brooks. Her dad, Layton, was my mentor from church. And her mom, Amy, is my interior decorator." They shook hands and Peter said goodbye, hopped over the banister onto the grass, and headed for his pickup.

"Do you have time to look around?" Parker asked Brianne.

"Sure. I was hoping you'd ask." She paused for dramatic effect. "This is the porch."

Parker laughed and followed her through the front door, leaning the package against the wall.

"And this must be the living room. I see couches and chairs. And bean bags?" She laughed. "And across the hall—oh, a bay window in the dining room. My parents have one I adore." She wandered past the large table into the big kitchen at the back of the house.

"I thought I was showing you around," Parker protested, as Brianne opened cabinet doors and inspected the walk-in pantry. The wood cabinets, cleaned of layers of paint, fairly glistened in the midday light coming through the windows and screen door.

"This must have been a very fine house. What's out there?" She pointed to weathered brick steps leading to a brick building.

"That was a carriage house in its day," Parker told her. "We'll have our group meetings and Bible studies there. It's got its own kitchenette, laundry, and bathroom. That staircase leads to what used to be servants' quarters on the second floor. I've made it a bedroom suite for my assistant."

Brianne continued past the kitchen door and a small bathroom off the hallway. Parker steered her from there to an area behind the living room. "My office," Parker explained. "Do you want to see the bedrooms upstairs?"

"Maybe later. I've got a thesis to finish." After a brief silence, she asked, "Parker, aren't you a little worried about the neighborhood?"

Parker's eyebrows shot up. He started to assure her about the renovation going on in this part of East Nashville, but he couldn't deny its reputation completely. Finally, he simply acknowledged that this ministry would need a lot of prayer support.

"You've got it," Brianne promised, a bit of relief washing over her face. "Our whole church will be praying!"

Parker moved into The Sloan House about a month before the residents were to begin arriving. Although he could afford the finest furnishings, Parker opted instead to choose items that would make the residents feel comfortable. Amy Brooks had understood his reasoning.

Together they shopped garage sales and discount stores, scouring Nashville for furniture and housewares. Local artists donated the wall art—everything from abstract to impressionistic to landscapes. Amy put everything together in a style she laughingly called "faux random."

The exceptions were the dining room's antique maple sideboard, table, and chairs and Parker's bedroom furniture, which he had saved from the estate sale at Gram Sloan's Kentucky residence.

He had invited his mother to select pieces she might like to have before he made his choices. It was his first meeting with her since the trial that had awarded him the estate. Aside from a few strands of gray, Olivia Hamilton hadn't changed.

Aware that she was a guest in her mother's home—a home Parker now owned—she feigned interest in the turns his life had taken and his new ministry. She appeared to look beyond him rather than at him as he talked. Occasionally asking a follow-up question or uttering an appreciative, "Oh, how nice," she maintained her distance, a distance Parker felt too keenly.

"I hope someday the family will visit The Sloan House," he offered. "I hope Father will get past his feelings about me—"

"Oh, I'm sure he will," his mother interrupted, unconvincingly. "Let's just give it some time."

Parker knew he would need help running The Sloan House. He'd prayed about hiring someone he could train in support group ministry similar to the way Connor had trained him. Someone who had a passion for men with a past and a hope for a glorious future in Christ.

Several months ago a name surfaced, seemingly out of nowhere. He first brushed the thought aside. Then, savoring the idea, he called his good friend Chaplain Jake. "Sure, I hear from him occasionally," Jake responded. "I think it's a great idea. The last I knew, he was doing some kind of street ministry in Miami. His mom passed away last October."

"Oh, I'm sorry to hear that." Parker copied the information Jake gave him, paused for a quick prayer, and punched in the phone number. Impatiently, Parker waited for the answer he so wanted to hear.

After three rings, a husky and familiar voice answered. "Malcolm, this is Parker Hamilton. Say, have I got a deal for you!"

By the time the first resident of The Sloan House arrived in April, Malcolm was settled in the bedroom suite above the meeting rooms in the former carriage house. His reunion with Parker had entailed a lot of whooping and hollering as they recounted Parker's struggles to understand Malcolm, his former cellie. Then, they praised God for bringing the two brothers in Christ back together in such an unlikely way.

Malcolm recounted that he'd been committed to his street ministry. But in truth, when Parker called, he was practically broke and homeless himself. The call had come at Malcolm's lowest point. Now, with Parker's job offer and the opportunity to learn new ministry skills, Malcolm could barely contain his joy. He'd already made the rounds in the neighborhood, telling everyone how Jesus had changed his life.

In his heart, Parker had a dream as to how Malcolm's story would play out someday. He would establish a second halfway house. The Amelia Winton House in Miami would be headed by her son, Malcolm. He'd keep that dream to himself for now.

But he needed one more position. He realized he couldn't keep up with The Sloan Foundation, fundraising engagements, and his role as mentor to the young men who would come and go from The Sloan House without some administrative help. When he mentioned this prayer request to Layton Brooks, he reminded Parker that Brianne Brooks would graduate in May with her master's degree in business administration from Belmont University.

When Parker approached her about the position, she agreed to help him until he found the right person. She'd keep her options open. He knew he might not have her long. Fortunately, Brianne proved a natural at keeping up with ordering, expenditures, reports, scheduling, and the myriad details of the residents' needs. Keeping him abreast of his appointments and fundraising efforts was another major responsibility.

He paid her well, offering more as her skill set improved. Soon, she began learning the art of writing foundation grant requests. Although she worked out of her parents' home, technology kept the two of them in constant touch.

Now with his staff at least temporarily complete, Parker could devote more time to sharing his testimony with church groups, civic clubs, and students. A couple of articles about The Sloan House appeared in *The Tennessean* and area newspapers, which gave Parker more speaking engagements. He marveled at how God replaced his shyness with His power when Parker stood to give God glory for what He had done.

26

Despite his busy schedule, Parker continued to experience the insomnia that had plagued him for years. Now without the relief offered by drugs, Parker decided to put the aimless hours staring at the ceiling to good use. He volunteered to be on call for a crisis intervention center. Parker considered the crisis calls, which invariably came in the early morning hours, his way of redeeming the time he lay awake, unable to sleep.

One night long after midnight, the phone rang. The crisis intervention center volunteer said someone was asking for him by name. "Put the call through," Parker said.

"So, bro, you got this God thing all figured out, huh?" Parker could tell the caller was drunk. He had learned most of these men simply needed to talk, so he listened for what would probably be a barrage of expletives and a hard luck story.

"Hey, Parker, you there?" Something about the voice sent his heart racing. A slow smile spread across his face. *God,* he prayed silently, *You are amazing! How can I ever thank You?*

The phone call lasted well into the wee hours of the morning. Parker's support group leader training helped him to listen, avoid giving advice, and wait through what seemed like eons of time as his brother Gavin floated in and out of coherency. Parker could also hear the swigs of whatever concoction Gavin was drinking.

Some commotion in the background—a scuffle perhaps—ended the call. Parker redialed the number and listened to a polished version of Gavin's recorded message giving instructions to leave a message.

"Gavin, it's Parker." Suddenly he couldn't think of a thing to say. 'Call me back,' seemed a little lame. 'Hey, enjoyed the conversation,' would be a lie. What he desperately wanted was to reach out in love—God's love—to this wandering sheep, who at some level wanted to be found and brought home. Why else would Gavin have brought up the subject of God?

So he said it. "Gavin, God loves you, and so do I. Let's meet—you name it. Anytime, anywhere. Give me a call." Parker left his number before ending the message. Suddenly, he felt exhausted. Sleep came quickly.

Meeting Gavin at a discreet location would have been far too easy, Parker surmised. Instead, Gavin continued his barrage of late-night calls, railing against most everything. Most amazing were Gavin's rants against him as the sole recipient of Gram Sloan's money. In Parker's battle with his father over his grandmother's will, he'd never stopped to consider the effect on his siblings. Did they think they had a claim to the inheritance, or at least to a portion of it?

He had always wondered why Gavin had never seemed much interested in cultivating a relationship with Gram. Who had he gone to with skinned knees, or shown his collection of treasures from an afternoon's play in the acreage surrounding the house? Who had he convinced to keep his frogs or butterflies in jars on the windowsill, at least until he could be persuaded to return them to nature? Now it seemed Gavin mourned a loss—not of relationship but of money.

Gavin also raged against his parents—parents who, from Parker's perspective, had showered him with every advantage. Parker had never entertained the possibility that Hollister's overbearing need for control and Olivia's studied indifference might have affected Gavin and Alexis as well. Parker had judged his siblings too harshly, he concluded, not taking into account that a dysfunctional family is dysfunctional to each individual in it. Gavin had gaping emotional wounds that he salved with alcohol and drugs—much as Parker had done. With this understanding came a new compassion and humility.

"God shapes us with a refiner's fire." The words from Pastor Frank's most recent sermon leaped to mind. "The Almighty uses different kilns with different temperatures for each of us. Don't judge your life as too hard or someone else's as too soft. Life isn't over 'til it's over," he added, "and you can quote me on that." The congregation chuckled.

"God knows how much pressure to bring to bear to achieve His purposes—ultimately to fashion us into the likeness of Christ. How much did Christ suffer to become our Savior? Should God require less of us?"

Parker didn't know the sacrifices Christ would yet require of him. He just knew that the strain of relating to Gavin was wearing him down emotionally and physically.

27

Brianne Brooks managed to effortlessly combine her part-time employment at the Sloan Foundation with a frustrating permanent job hunt. For now, she liked the investment she was making in people's lives. She woke with a sense of purpose and loved the opportunity to pray with and for her coworkers and the residents. Each successful graduation was a testimony of God's power to give His followers new life in Christ.

When Brianne would drop by with papers to sign or other business, the three employees—Parker, Malcolm, and Brianne—would gather in Parker's small office for prayer. With some difficulty, Brianne would join the men on her knees. She almost never gave her prosthesis a thought. It was her trophy of grace, a reminder that she survived two bouts with childhood cancer. Also, God had used the circumstances to bring her divorced parents back together again.

Parker regularly asked for their prayers for Gavin. On one such occasion, Brianne shared a picture that came to mind. "I see a gray-haired lady in a simple house dress, browned from years outdoors, with a sunbeam smile, a word of hope, and the same bright blue eyes shared by her daughter and granddaughter.

"My Meme Dyer is the most fervent prayer warrior I know. She has a way of listening to God and sensing when He's at work in an individual's heart. 'God's up to something,' she'll say. The phrase has become the family mantra. I'll ask Meme to pray for Gavin."

As Malcolm prayed for God's victory in Gavin's life, he reminded them that forces from above vied for Gavin's soul. Malcolm quoted straight from

Ephesians 6:12 in the King James Bible that his mom, Amelia Winton, had read to him each night before bedtime. "For we wrestle not against flesh and blood, but against principalities, against powers, against the rulers of the darkness of this world, against spiritual wickedness in high places."

Today, as Malcolm prayed, Brianne whispered to God, "I trust you *are* up to something in Gavin's life. Please help us all to walk by faith."

Parker found himself mentioning Gavin to most everyone he encountered who seemed to evidence a praying heart. At night the eight residents who now occupied The Sloan House included Gavin in their prayer times. Pastor Frank offered prayer support, as well as the men's prayer group Layton Brooks attended. As the days became months, Parker's faith began to waver. "God, give me hope. I need some assurance that You are listening."

God answered his prayer in a most unexpected way when he answered his ringing phone.

"Parker, could you fill in for me tonight?"

Parker barely recognized the raspy voice on the other end of the phone. "Ted Poole? What's a doctor doing getting sick?"

Ted sneezed and blew his nose. "The common cold. Haven't had one in years."

Parker tried to suppress a grin at the thought that his buff friend, who jogged every morning rain or shine, had been felled by a microscopic villain. "What can I do for you?"

Ted supplied the details in as few words as possible. Tonight was the annual awards banquet for the Young Lawyers Club, and he was in no shape to deliver a speech accepting an award on behalf of the medical clinic. Could Parker do him the favor?

"Tell 'em we appreciate their victims' rights and legal defense work for our patients at the clinic. Ask 'em to volunteer on the legal hot line." Ted coughed and asked Susan to bring him some water. "Plug the medical clinic. Oh, yeah, and don't forget The Sloan House."

"Like that would happen!" Parker checked his schedule. Malcolm could lead the Bible study group at The Sloan House for him. "Sure, I'll be glad to. But —"

"I know what you're thinking," Ted volunteered as he took a sip of water. "You don't have the warmest relationship with the Nashville legal community. Thank you, Hollister Hamilton! But I already tried several others, and you're my last hope."

"Thanks for the compliment," Parker retorted. After Ted hung up, Parker alerted Malcolm to the change in plans, quickly showered and changed, and headed toward Broadway and the downtown hotel—all the while wondering if attorney Gavin Hamilton might be among the attendees.

28

Parker saw Gavin enter the hotel ballroom with a drink in hand. Taking a seat at a back table, Gavin never glanced toward the head table, absorbed instead with the small group of men and women seated around him. He looked thin—yet handsome—with his dark hair and eyes.

Shorter than Parker, he was still a commanding figure and seemed to take charge of the conversation around the table. In the dimly lit room, Parker couldn't make out much more. He knew the chances of Gavin staying around after he spoke were nil, so he turned to the emcee, a lawyer from Hollister Hamilton's law firm. Parker had known him from high school.

"Hayden, do me a favor, ok?"

"Sure, Parker. What do you need?"

"Find a reason for Gavin to stay a minute after the banquet. I've got to talk to him while he's moderately sober."

Whether he understood the urgency in Parker's voice, he agreed. Moments later, he excused himself from the head table and moved among the crowd, shaking hands and bantering with several he had faced in court. Gradually, he drifted to Gavin's table. Parker felt the familiar red flush creep up his neck. He awkwardly struck up a conversation with the man on his right, the incoming president of the organization.

When the meal was served, Parker picked at his food, trying to get his head around what he would say to the gathering. Foremost in his mind was what he'd say to Gavin if he got the chance. When Parker was introduced as the guest speaker, Gavin's eyes met his briefly but dropped quickly to the floor. A guy seated next to Gavin nudged him and appeared to ask a question. Gavin shook his head and waved off the expected answer.

Parker stumbled a bit through his remarks and sat down to a smattering of applause. Now what? he thought anxiously. Immediately the instructions of St. Paul in Colossians 3:15 came to mind: *Let God's peace control your heart.*

"I'm not saying it went well," Parker told Malcolm as they sat across from each other in the living room of The Sloan House. "I wish I'd said some things I didn't and hadn't said some things I did."

"God uses even crooked sticks," Malcolm encouraged. "Think of all the heroes of faith in the Bible. Not a one of them got everything right every time."

"I know, I know. I'd just planned in my mind how this first meeting would go, and this was nothing like what I'd imagined."

"So, what did Gavin say?" Malcolm queried.

"Nothing."

"Nothing?"

"Absolutely nothing. He stood like a caged animal waiting to be let out. I only had a few minutes with him. Then a friend of his passed by. He mumbled an excuse and left. I told him I'd be at the Vantage Point tomorrow night around 10.

"The club on Second Avenue?"

"Yeah, I thought meeting on neutral ground might help. We'll see if he shows."

"Fat chance of that happening," Malcolm replied. "It would take a miracle of God."

Parker sat with a club soda in a booth at the back of the Vantage Point. Ten o'clock became 10:30, then 11:00. Parker resolved to give Gavin until midnight, although he didn't have much hope his brother would still be sober at that hour.

At 12:15 Parker stood and took some bills from his wallet. He was about to lay them on the table when he saw Gavin enter the club and look around. Parker sat back down.

Parker and Gavin were meeting fairly regularly now. Their conversations exhausted Parker. He sometimes wondered why he'd even tried to reestablish a relationship with him. Gavin had a definite chip on his shoulder, and he seemed to believe he could take out all his frustrations on his older brother.

In truth, he could—to a certain extent. Parker had been trained to listen. Not to react in anger. Not to give advice except when asked. In addition, he daily sought God's wisdom, as promised in James 1:5. Occasionally, he delivered a piercing question or uttered a statement Gavin probably hadn't considered. Was he making a dent in his defenses?

Surely, God wouldn't have brought him into regular contact with his brother for Gavin to continue to resist Him forever. No, God had a purpose to these encounters. Just as Parker waited, the God of Heaven was waiting for Gavin to come to the end of his resources and look upward.

29

Parker wanted to continue his progress through The Twelve Steps of Alcoholics Anonymous. He'd lost his sponsor when he'd left the halfway house in Orlando. Not surprisingly, Malcolm had been through the program and offered his help. He resumed step eight: *made a list of all persons we had harmed, and became willing to make amends to them all.* Parker knew each of his family members had reasons to feel he had harmed them.

First, he knew he'd have to be willing to give up everything if it meant winning his family to Christ. Would Gram's money ever be a nonissue to his parents, brother, and sister? Yet The Sloan House, Malcolm, and the eight current residents were depending on The Sloan Foundation for survival. Could he—should he—jeopardize their futures for an unknown outcome?

Parker had to think long and hard about his obligations, but he was finally able to pray that God would strip him of any possession that would take his eyes off the goal. *I need a stash of faith in God and in me,* he reminded himself.

After many conversations with Pastor Frank and countless prayers on his and Malcolm's part, Parker concluded that God wasn't asking him to give up Gram's inheritance. Somehow, He would use it to bring some or all of his family to faith in Christ.

Slowly, he began writing letters asking for forgiveness. Alexis' reply brushed aside his carefully worded apology sent to a villa in Italy, which she shared with the son of a wealthy art dealer in Milan. *I don't need your money,* it read, *and you don't need my forgiveness. Get over yourself, Parker. It's not that big a deal. I'll bring Eduardo to meet the family one of these days. Love ya, Alexis.*

Parker's mother had responded on embossed letterhead in beautiful cursive. *Dear Parker, I know how Gram loved you. She never lost hope of seeing you again. And I know how very proud she would be of The Sloan House. I appreciate your honoring her memory in this way. Let's get together soon, all right? Love, Mother.*

Parker felt the insincerity of her invitation, but he crossed another name off his list. At least his mother wasn't interested in pursuing her lost fortune. Hollister, on the other hand, never responded to Parker' letter. He pursed his lips. *Wonder if I should try a singing telegram?* The thought made him laugh out loud.

Parker continued to write people from his past who lived too far away to visit. He met personally with those in Nashville, including former friends and professors. His apologies were always accepted, if not totally understood. Soon he would talk to Gavin about Gram's money. When the time was right.

Step 9 was a caution: *made direct amends to such people wherever possible, except when to do so would injure them or others.* Step-by-step, always proceeding with caution, ever seeking the will of God. This Christian life he was leading wasn't getting any easier.

Several weeks had passed without a word from Gavin. One night Parker called his cell phone but got no answer. He felt a strange urge, as though he were being compelled to go to Gavin's condo and check on him. *God, if this is from You, give me a way to get into his place.*

At Gavin's condo, Parker approached the desk and asked the attendant to ring Gavin. When there was no answer, he tried to sound casual. "I saw his car in the parking garage. He must be taking a shower or something."

He pulled out his identification. "I'm Gavin's brother, Parker. I'd really like to surprise him. It's been a while since we've seen each other. Do you think I might go up and knock on his door? I think if he heard my voice, he'd open right up." He pulled a few bills from his wallet and slid them across the desk.

"Well," said the attendant, "If you're sure he'd want to see you. I assume you know his unit number. Elevator is straight ahead." He punched a button to release the elevator lock.

Parker had a vague remembrance of Gavin's floor and unit. If he got the number wrong, he wondered how he would explain his presence. He found the unit but his knocks produced no response. Prison had contributed a few skills to his life, so he picked the lock. If no one was home, no harm done. If so, well, he'd cross that bridge when he came to it.

Cautiously, he opened the door. Gavin lay on the floor of the living room. He rushed to him, checked his vitals, and called 9-1-1. The paramedics arrived and stabilized him before whisking him away to the hospital. Parker gathered a few toiletries and a change of underwear and socks and headed to the hospital.

He stayed as close to Gavin's side as the staff would allow. As he'd assumed, Gavin had overdosed. Parker thanked God that He had nudged him to his brother's side just in the nick of time.

30

Gavin regained consciousness shortly before dawn. Parker gave him a short synopsis of how he'd wound up in the hospital. "Don't tell Dad," he pleaded. "I'll—I'll call in sick."

"You're going home with me," Parker insisted. "You're not doing this drug thing anymore, bro." Too weak to protest, Gavin allowed himself to be released into Parker's care.

Malcolm took charge of the situation as soon as Gavin felt able to keep food on his stomach. He was simply more "street smart" than Parker and kept Gavin under strict surveillance. Eventually, Gavin's drug cravings subsided to the point that he and Parker could talk about the future. Although he worried some about his caseload at the office, his disappearance hadn't caused great alarm. Apparently, the law firm was accustomed to it.

"Gavin, you can continue down the road you've been taking and wind up dead, or you can give yourself another chance at life." Parker paused. "You know where I stand. You know what I stand for. I'll help you any way I can." After some serious soul-searching, Gavin checked himself in to a drug rehab facility not far from Nashville. Hollister didn't seem fazed by the news. What was one more drug rehab bill if he could get the help he needed? He said he would cover for him at work.

Parker participated in several of Gavin's rehab therapy sessions—since none of the rest of the family wanted to be involved. On his release from the facility—drug free and physically healthier than ever—Gavin asked

Parker the question his brother had been praying he would ask once again. "So, bro, you got this God thing figured out?"

Gavin leaned back in his office chair and stretched. He had been clean of drugs and alcohol for more than five months. He was still getting used to his body, to sensations he hadn't felt in a long time. In some ways, life seemed tougher. In other ways, he felt good about himself and his future.

After being discharged by the rehab facility, he'd stayed at Parker's for a while to avoid temptation. He'd participated in the recovery groups and Bible studies at The Sloan House. Guided by the loving counsel of his brother, his transition from sinner to saint took only months. He voiced the sinner's prayer and experienced God's cleansing grace. However, he knew he had a lifetime of bad habits to break—with power from above.

As he snapped back to the present, he heard noise in the office hallway. Some of his colleagues planned to meet at one of the nearby watering spots for happy hour. They no longer invited Gavin. Suddenly, he remembered he had homework for the Bible study that evening at The Sloan House. What was the passage? Some guy's first name?

Gavin often confused the four gospel writers. "How do you tell them apart?" he had quizzed Parker soon after he became a Christian. "Which of them knew Jesus when He was alive? Which was first?" Parker either patiently answered his questions or pointed him to a reference source.

Today it seemed easier to just ask him. He dialed his number.

Parker picked up the call. "Luke chapter 15," he volunteered. After he hung up, he strolled from his office into the kitchen where Malcolm was chopping carrots on a cutting board. "Hey Malcolm, Gavin wants one of your BLTs when he comes to the Bible study tonight. Said he wouldn't have a chance to eat beforehand. Is that ok?"

"Not a problem. Except I don't know why he calls it a BLT. He always takes off the lettuce."

Parker grinned and turned back to his office to finish his preparation for the Bible study. Gavin's questions were endless, not unlike Parker's in prison when he would harangue Malcolm after lights out. But Gavin caught on quickly. Probably too smart for his own good, Parker surmised.

Gavin had had the world at his feet—good looks, wealthy family, education, a prestigious career—but none of it had satisfied him. Unlike Hollister, who grabbed for every morsel life had to offer, Gavin had tasted and spit it out. Drugs and alcohol barely camouflaged Gavin's disdain for everything that had been handed him on the proverbial silver platter.

Parker mentally reviewed their first faltering attempts at talking to each other. The phone conversations had always ended in Gavin's angry outbursts. Almost everything had triggered his quick temper. Gavin still had a short fuse, but he'd made so much progress, in every way.

The thought of a relationship with his brother still overwhelmed him. He turned to his Bible and looked up Luke 15 and read verse 10: "I tell you, in the same way, there is joy in the presence of God's angels over one sinner who repents."

31

"But, Pops, you have to at least see Parker," Gavin exploded.

"I do not have to do anything! And don't call me Pops," Hollister Hamilton groused from behind his massive mahogany desk.

"Why do you have to be like this?" Gavin threw up his hands in exasperation and stomped out of his father's office, slamming the door behind him as he stomped into Ruby's office.

Parker sat waiting across from his father's secretary's desk. He glanced up from a magazine. "Looks like it didn't go so well."

"Yeah, you could say that."

Parker could almost see steam coming from his brother's nostrils.

"Let's go."

"Nice to see you, Ruby," Parker called as he followed his brother down the hall and into his cramped and cluttered office. His desk lay buried beneath stacks of files. He sat in his swivel chair and motioned for Parker to take the other chair across from him.

"He's the most stubborn man on the planet." Gavin ran his hands through his black hair, as though this would be news to Parker. "It's not like you'd been on death row."

"Believe me, I get it." Parker sighed. "We took a chance. It just didn't pay off, that's all. Father will come around eventually. I'm sure of it."

"Well, I'm not so sure he wants to see me, much less you. If I didn't have so many cases pending, he'd probably shove me right out the door."

After a brief silence, Parker stood. "Will I see you tonight?"

"Yeah, I'll be there."

Parker looked back from the doorway. "Thanks for trying."

"Sure, no problem." Gavin picked up a file and with a mouse click was back in the world of corporate real estate law.

Malcolm was hand washing some pots too large for the dishwasher when Parker entered from the kitchen door. He looked up. "How'd it go?" he asked.

"Could've gone better," his boss stated matter-of-factly.

Malcolm dried his hands and sat down on a stool at the serving island. "Tell me about it."

Sitting beside him, Parker described the failed attempt. "My father wouldn't see me. Gavin made this big production out of it. But I told him it was ok. I wasn't really expecting a teary-eyed reunion."

"Sorry, man." Malcolm looked down at his sneakers. There didn't seem to be much else to say. "Well, let's take one major answer to prayer at a time. Don't forget you've got a brother who's a brother in Christ!" Malcolm laughed at his play on words.

"You're absolutely right. Major answer to prayer." After Parker disappeared around the corner, Malcolm returned to the sink, back to praying and praising as he dried one pot, then another. "Father God, I praise You for Your faithfulness and the difference it's making in Gavin's life. Thank You, thank You, glory halleluiah!"

Soon after Gavin became a Christian, Parker asked him to consider being mentored by Layton Brooks. He said it was a family tradition—or it would be as soon as Gavin agreed. It had taken several months to get on Layton's waiting list, but now he met with him weekly.

Layton was a pro at getting guys to talk. He'd had plenty of practice with Ted Poole, Parker, and a string of guys before them. The fellows he mentored became the sons he'd never had.

Soon into their relationship Gavin found himself sharing experiences and seeking insight about events he'd not been aware had affected him deeply. Slowly, they'd moved toward discussing his family dynamics. His recap was much different from Parker's since they'd had very different experiences.

Gavin met Layton at the IHOP for breakfast. Having a morning meal at all was a new experience for Gavin, much less being accountable to a middle-aged guy in a golf shirt, shorts, and loafers. Today, when he pulled into a parking space, Gavin stuffed his tie in his coat pocket. He'd need it later for court.

When the hour was up, the two of them walked toward the parking lot. A young woman in a square cut car pulled up beside them. "Hey, Dad," she called.

Layton grinned. "I'm ready, Kitten." He turned to Gavin. "My daughter's going to follow me to the car dealership to leave my car for servicing. Have you met her?"

"The famous Brianne Brooks?' He moved toward her open car window. "Sure. I've seen her at Parker's house."

Brianne's brilliant blue eyes always seemed to cut through Gavin's exterior, leaving him feeling exposed and vulnerable. "Hi, Gavin. I'm so pleased to hear you're a believer now. That's great!"

"Yeah." The young lawyer couldn't think of anything else to say. But he wished she'd stop looking at him.

"Hey," Brianne continued, "The singles at our church are getting together Friday night for a cookout. Want to come?"

Church was still a big hurdle for him. So far he'd only attended worship services. "Sure," Gavin heard himself saying. "When and where?"

Later, as he reflected on his response, Gavin wondered, *Where had it come from? Why did I agree to that?* He grumbled as he entered the courtroom.

32

Friday night at the cookout Gavin stayed near Brianne, prepared to be put off by these Bible thumping believers. Brianne mingled effortlessly, introducing him to all her friends with an off-hand, "Gavin, Parker Hamilton's brother." She left him to fill in any blanks he wished. The singles all knew Parker from church. Several asked about the ministry.

At first, Gavin wasn't sure what *the ministry* meant. Brianne bailed him out. "The Sloan House is going very well, thank you. We've graduated sixteen clients so far."

Just then, the back gate to the lawn opened, and Gavin heard shouts of "Hi, Pastor Frank." The balding man walked over to a cluster of singles and began talking.

"Have you met our minister?" Brianne asked.

"Not officially," he said.

Soon Pastor Frank ambled their way. Brianne took his arm and ushered him toward the minister. "I'd like you to meet Gavin Hamilton."

Pastor Frank was all smiles. "Gavin, what a delight." The older man seemed to be taking his measure. "I've seen you with Parker, but you don't look much like him."

"No, he favors the Sloans, my mother's side of the family." Gavin tried to stare down the kindly face, much as he would in court, but the minister held his gaze.

"Gavin, I'd love to meet you for lunch someday. What's the name of that sandwich shop on the first floor of your firm's building? I don't get downtown as much as I used to, but I recall eating there once."

Gavin stood as though planted in concrete. A million excuses popped into his mind, but he couldn't seem to get any of them out.

"That's a wonderful idea," Brianne beamed. "Isn't it, Gavin?"

Stupefied by his own lack of nerve, Gavin heard himself say, "Sure." The two men exchanged business cards and promised to get in touch. Meanwhile, Brianne had wandered over to visit with another group of friends. She glanced back at Gavin and winked.

What's that supposed to mean? he wondered.

Settled at a table in the coffee shop, Gavin ordered a BLT sandwich. "Hold the lettuce," he told the server.

"I'll take the Reuben, no fries, thank you." Pastor Frank put down his menu as the server disappeared behind the counter. "My wife, Myra, never approved of a Reuben sandwich. Said it had too much fat and too many calories. A man's got to live a little," he laughed.

Gavin smiled, then mustered a sincere, "I was sorry to hear about your wife."

"Huge loss. Even after all these years, I still expect her to greet me at the front door when I come home."

He was surprised by the minister's candor. Somehow he had expected his reply to be full of pious words about God's will. The server brought their soft drinks and straws. Gavin took his first sip.

"So, Gavin, tell me how you met the Lord."

Soft drink spewed everywhere as Gavin began choking. Other diners turned. Gavin coughed into his napkin.

"Are you ok?" Pastor Frank began mopping up drops from the table, unaware that he'd asked Gavin anything out of the ordinary.

After the coughing subsided, their orders arrived. Gavin attacked his sandwich with vigor. By then, Pastor Frank had launched into his views on the age-old rivalry between Vanderbilt University and Gavin's alma mater, the University of Tennessee.

"You ever watch them play basketball at Memorial Gym?"

Gavin was on familiar turf. He breathed a sigh of relief.

At their next meeting, which Brianne insisted was only polite, Gavin extended the invitation. They ate at a more secluded place, a booth in a posh restaurant on Broadway. "My treat," Gavin had explained.

They were halfway through their salads when once again Pastor Frank asked about his new faith. This time he was better prepared for the minister's spiritual probing. Gavin told the story.

"I had passed out on my living room floor from a drug overdose. Parker called my cell phone. He left a message about us getting together. When I didn't call him back, he had this gut feeling that something wasn't right. That night, God knew I needed help. I think He told Parker I was in trouble.

"Parker saw my car in the parking lot at my condo and took that as I sign I was home. He sweet-talked the desk guy at the building into letting him take the elevator to my floor. Told him he was my long-lost brother here to surprise me. True enough," he chuckled.

Gavin took a sip of water. "After banging on the door several times, he picked my lock." At the minister's look of surprise, he smiled. "Parker saw no use in ignoring all those tricks he picked up in prison years ago. Anyway, there I was on the floor. Parker checked my vitals and called 9-1-1."

"You were smart to have a doctor for a brother."

Gavin grinned. "Yes, I was. In the ER every time I'd regain consciousness, I'd see Parker's face. I kept wondering what he was doing there. Nothing going on around me made sense. When I was discharged, he took me home with him. Put me in his bed and slept on the floor beside me. You might say that made me more willing to listen to him share his faith in Christ. I kept waiting for the old defenses to go up. But Someone was getting through all the garbage."

Pastor Frank nodded. "So characteristic of God to show Himself when you were flat on your back. I often find that to be the case."

"After rehab, I accepted Christ as my Savior. You might say I had a few questions. Now I'm trying to figure out how to live like Jesus."

Pastor Frank frowned. "That could be a problem."

"What do you mean?"

"I'd advise you to know Jesus instead. No 'like Jesus' about it."

Now Gavin was confused. The minister pressed on. "It's a relationship, Gavin. You don't learn to be like me in order to build our relationship. You learn about me. We share our lives with each other.

"Being like Jesus is a by-product of being with Jesus. Back in the day, folks would talk about how much Myra and I were alike. Didn't start out that way, but we grew to enjoy the same things. In a similar way, keep talking to Jesus. Ask Him questions. Do what He tells you. In due time He'll answer all those issues of what to keep in your life and what to discard. Believe me, He'll show you."

Gavin squirmed at the idea of not knowing on the front end. "That's tough," he admitted.

"We call it the way of faith." Pastor Frank gave him a tender smile. "I'm here to help in any way I can."

33

A few days later, Brianne called her new friend. "Hey, Gavin, the singles class is starting a new Bible study this Sunday. How about coming?"

Gavin literally scratched his head. "Well, um, I'd like to, but—"

"How do you know you won't like it if you don't come?" she countered.

Feeling trapped, he sat down on his couch and rested his feet on the coffee table. "I don't get this church stuff. A bunch of people get together in their nice clothes—"

"It's not like that," Brianne interrupted. "It's—it's more like boot camp."

"Pardon me?"

"Oh, you know what I mean," a touch of exasperation in her tone. "We get together to train, to prepare for battle, to build troop morale."

"I was never in the military."

"Well, you are now." Brianne insisted he get out his Bible. "Turn to Ephesians 6."

After finding the book tucked behind Galatians, he flipped to chapter six. Brianne read verses 10–20 aloud. She reviewed the various pieces of spiritual armor. "We're in a war, Gavin. We have an enemy. We need each other's strength."

He had no ready comeback to that argument. He agreed to meet her at 9:30 Sunday morning.

One evening six months later, Parker concluded the Bible study session at The Sloan House. One by one the men ambled over to the main house to their rooms for the night. Gavin rested on a floor pillow, enjoying a moment alone with his big brother.

Malcolm had offered to make them some hot tea. Now he brought them steaming cups and set them on an end table between the two men. "Night, guys," he waved as he headed for his quarters up the back stairs.

"Goodnight, Malcolm," Parker called after him. With a mischievous look on his face, he asked Gavin, "Want to know a secret?"

"Sure. Always up for a secret."

"I'd like to help Malcolm get a halfway house going in Miami."

Gavin whistled. "Tough place!"

Parker nodded. "It will take a chunk of Gram's money. We've never talked about that—about the inheritance. I guess I've been afraid to bring it up."

Gavin sat in silence for a minute. He took a sip of tea. "I'll admit, I was mad about it at first. Well, to be honest, for a long time." He stretched his long legs. "Now that I've seen what you're doing here and what the potential is for other druggies like me to meet Jesus, well—it's different now. I wouldn't have it any other way."

Parker bowed his head; a tear trickled down his cheek.

"You cry at the drop of a hat," Gavin scolded.

"Sorry, bro." But he wasn't. He wiped his face with a tissue from a box on the end table. Long ago, he'd learned to be comfortable with his tears—and keep tissue on hand.

"I plan to talk to Malcolm about it soon. I'm praying he'll be open to the idea." He paused. "I've got to ask you something else. Mr. Tomlin is retiring."

A grin spread across Gavin's face. "I know. I'm getting his office."

"It's about time you moved from that pigeon-hole you're in."

"Never wanted to pack up my stuff before. So what about it?"

"I'd like for you to be The Sloan Foundation's attorney. I'm not asking for full time or to give up your other clients at the law firm. Just add me to your long list of people clamoring for your attention. For one thing, I want to keep the door open to our parents."

Gavin scratched his chin, as though debating the issue. "I can do that. I'll try not to embezzle too much."

Parker poked him in the ribs.

"And another thing. Once Malcolm leaves for Miami, I'll need help. Gavin, you've got a gift for explaining things. You've been where most of our residents are. I think you'd do a great job leading one of our support groups and, eventually, a Bible study. I'd be willing to train you. Just like Connor and Megan trained me and I trained Malcolm. Think about it. Pray about it." Parker's plea was intense, unusual in their comfortable relationship.

A few weeks later the two brothers again sat cross-legged on the floor of the carriage house, debriefing the latest support group meeting. Gavin drew his legs up and leaned in toward Parker. "This Bible study Brianne is making me go to," he began.

They both laughed at the thought of Brianne's take-charge ways.

"We just studied about Simon Peter and Andrew leaving their nets to follow Jesus."

"Yeah?"

"Here." Gavin handed him something imaginary. "Take my net. I won't be needing it anymore."

Parker's eyebrows shot up. "Meaning?"

"I'm in, bro. Teach me all you've got."

34

Parker swelled with pride as he observed Gavin leading his first Bible study. Over the past few months his brother had made impressive strides toward becoming a valuable member of The Sloan House team. Parker had enrolled him in several online Bible classes. They also attended a support group leader training event in Atlanta and a local one in Nashville. Gavin—along with Parker—completed his Twelve Steps program through Alcoholics Anonymous. Finally, he met Beryl, the first person that would call him his AA sponsor.

Gavin continued to meet with Layton Brooks on a regular basis. Parker respected the privacy of a mentor-mentee relationship and never asked questions about their time together. He, too, had been in the same kind of intimate relationship with Layton and still sought his counsel on major decisions. How he praised God for answering his prayers for his brother, who was a brother in Christ.

Meanwhile, Parker put into motion the plans for a halfway house in Miami, Florida. He hadn't shared the proposal with Malcolm. He wanted to make sure the feasibility study came back with a positive reply. Brianne had done a lot of the legwork and promised to keep her lips sealed.

Ah, Brianne. What a find she had turned out to be. She thrived on grant writing, inventory, ordering, and other details that drove Parker insane. Her hours had increased to fulltime. Since getting her master's degree, she claimed to be waiting for the perfect job to come along. He found no reason to think she was actively looking. He told himself she'd found her calling.

His primary concern was Gavin's schedule. His brother already had a fulltime job with his father's law firm. He was The Sloan Foundation attorney. And now Parker had him leading groups several nights a week. Gavin definitely had a lot on his plate.

Parker bowed his head and silently prayed that God would protect Gavin from burnout. *I need wisdom, Lord. Please don't let me be the cause of him doing more than You've asked him to do.*

Today was the last mentoring session Layton Brooks would have with Gavin Hamilton. Usually, a final time together proved emotional. However, it didn't take a genius to tell that Gavin was nervous. With his mentoring history, Layton had been here before. Other young men had sat across from him with information they were reluctant to share. He waited patiently, sipping his coffee at the IHOP where they met.

Finally, Gavin lifted his eyes to meet those of his mentor. "I'm not sure how to say this," he began, shifting his weight in his chair. "But your daughter calls me a lot. We see each other at church, and—"

Layton sat quietly, keeping eye contact.

"Well, sir, I think she likes me." Gavin lowered his eyes.

"Oh, I'm sure she does," Layton replied. "She speaks highly of you. You've obviously grown in the Lord over this past year."

Gavin shook his head slightly. "No, that's not what I mean."

Layton looked perplexed. "Then, what do you mean?"

"Well," he stammered a little, "I-I think she wants me to ask her out. You know, like on a date."

Layton put his elbow on the table and held his chin in his hand. "And—you don't want to do that?"

"Oh, no sir, I mean, yes, I do. I mean, I'd be open to the idea."

"But something about *the idea* is troubling you?"

Gavin lowered his eyes again. "I was afraid it would trouble you."

"Say on," the older man prodded.

"I know you have high standards for Brianne. You've brought her up in the church, and she's light years ahead of me in knowing the Bible and sharing her faith and—

"Wait a minute, Gavin. Are you suggesting that I might not approve of your dating Brianne?"

Gavin mustered his last bit of courage. "You'd have every reason not to approve," he insisted.

"Because?"

Gavin looked confused. "You know my background as well as anyone. I've been very honest about my substance abuse. I've only been a Christian for a little more than a year. Frankly, sir, if anything were to come of my dating her, I-I don't deserve her." His eyes grew moist.

Layton looked up and studied the ceiling tiles. Gavin waited an interminable minute for him to say something. Finally, he spoke. "It seems we have a similar problem, Gavin. I don't deserve her either. In fact, I've often wondered why God ever entrusted her to my care.

"You didn't know me back when Brianne was little. I was a very selfish, arrogant person, feeling in control of my little part of the world—until that world started falling apart. When I came to grips with my own self-centeredness and with how I'd boxed God in to a space where I thought I controlled Him—well, I was a broken man.

"I didn't think I deserved Amy's forgiveness, and I certainly didn't feel proud of my role as a father. If both of them had told me 'goodbye and good luck,' I'd have understood." Layton paused and layered his hands on the table top.

"But God gave me a second chance as both a husband and father. I eventually stopped trying to deserve Amy and Brianne and learned to receive them as grace gifts from the Father. If I'd waited to feel adequate to be loved by them, I'd still be waiting."

Gavin took a moment to absorb what he'd heard. He ventured a summary. "So, are you saying you'd be all right with my dating her?"

"Well, let me ask you a few questions."

"Okay."

"Are you a new man in Christ?"

Gavin's eyes grew moist again. "Yes, sir, I am."

"Are you seeking to follow God with your heart, soul, and mind?"

"I am."

"Do you give priority to study of the Bible and supporting His church?"

"Yes."

"Do you intend to uphold the highest standards of purity in your dating relationships?

Gavin held his head high. "I will."

"Then, I'd be honored for you to date my daughter."

Several days later Gavin mustered enough courage to call Brianne. When she picked up the call, she sounded surprised and pleased. At that point, Gavin lost all recall as to what he planned to say.

As he thought about it later, he remembered very few times when circumstances had left him speechless. In those instances, he'd been caught red-handed in a prank, or some gorgeous girl had failed to immediately grasp how fortunate she'd be to go out with him.

His courtroom demeanor was master of the universe plus one. He'd often gone toe-to-toe with his overbearing father. He'd sweet-talked his way into many venues he shouldn't have been allowed to enter.

Then, there was Brianne. As he stood holding the phone in his hand, he could picture her piercing blue eyes staring into the inner sanctum of his heart. She'd know the power she held over him. Was he ready to be vulnerable with another human being? Especially a vivacious strawberry blonde who barely came to his shoulder yet made rational thought nearly impossible?

He awakened out of his thought bubble when she asked, "Gavin, are you still there?"

He recovered his voice in time to keep her from hanging up. "Sure, it's me. How are you?"

"Fine." He could hear the amusement in her voice.

"Good. That's good." He couldn't think of any small talk. "I was wondering if you'd like to go eat sometime. With me. Uh, maybe lunch." Surely, she wouldn't read too much into a lunch date.

"Sounds like fun. Or, did you need to talk to me about something?"

"No, no, just, ah, fun."

"Okay, when and where? Make it easy on my pocketbook."

Was she going to make him say it? He took a long breath. "I'm buying." They set a day, time, and place. Gavin felt a little queasy as he hung up.

35

Layton feigned surprise when Brianne dangled her keys in the doorway of his man cave and announced that she was meeting Gavin for lunch.

He'd just returned from his Saturday golf game and already had a professional golf game on his television screen. He looked up at her from his couch and asked, "Any special reason?"

She came into the room and plopped down on the arm of the couch. "I don't know. He didn't say."

"Well, you two have fun." Layton turned his attention back to the game. Brianne kissed his cheek and left the room. Soon he heard her car engine humming in the driveway.

Layton placed his elbows on his knees and folded his hands between them. The golf game seemed immaterial now. So, Gavin had taken the plunge and asked to meet Brianne for lunch? He had a feeling about how this relationship might play out. He bowed his head and prayed for wisdom for the young couple, just as James 1:5 had encouraged him to do: "Now if any of you lacks wisdom, he should ask God, who gives to all generously and without criticizing, and it will be given to him."

Then he went to find Amy. What was her take on the matter?

After his lunch with Brianne, Gavin headed for The Sloan House. On Saturday afternoons he met with Beryl as his AA sponsor. Beryl was stuck on Step 3: *Made a decision to turn our will and our lives over to the care of God as we understood Him.* His idea of a higher Power had not been one of a caring God. In fact, he'd believed the One who created the mess we were all in went off and left it. Anyone who thought this Power cared about him personally was delusional.

Having felt the same way most of his life, Gavin listened as Beryl tried to make a case for an impersonal Supreme Being. At some point, he would ask Gavin for his thoughts. For now, he needed to tell someone how a loving God surely wouldn't have placed him in an abusive home with such inattentive parents. Gavin said a silent prayer, thanking God that he was no longer stuck in the past, blaming others for all his bad choices.

When their time was up, Gavin ambled into the kitchen, where Malcolm already had burgers ready for the grill. Saturday night was always hamburgers with all the toppings. The rest of the week Malcolm trained the newbies in how to cook a square meat-and-three.

Malcolm grinned when Gavin came to the prep area to see what munchies were within reach. "How come you show up every Saturday night, just like the moon?" he asked.

"I work undercover for the health department," Gavin joked. "Checking the cleanliness of the place." He opened the refrigerator door and looked around. "Malcolm, you ever been married?"

"Can't say as I've been that lucky. I was barely old enough to vote before I did my time in the slammer. Haven't been able to work steady until now. Why? You got somebody for me?"

"Naw. Just wondered." He grazed on a couple of carrot sticks. "Ever been in love?"

Malcolm turned to stare at him. "Now this conversation is getting mighty interesting. You got the love bug?"

Gavin kept eating. "Not close. Wondered what it was like, that's all. Parker wouldn't have a clue. Doubt he's ever been on a date."

Malcolm nodded. "You're probably right about that. Guess you'll have to ask around. How about Mr. Layton Brooks? Now there's a happily married guy."

Gavin coughed up specks of carrot. His face flushed as he headed to the bathroom. He pointed to his mouth as if to explain his exit.

When she returned from lunch, Brianne found her mom in the kitchen making a pound cake for one of their elderly neighbors. "I get to lick the bowl," she announced. She pulled out a stool and sat down at the kitchen island.

Her mom grinned and moved the bowl a safe distance away. "Tell me about your lunch with Gavin. How did it go?"

Brianne chuckled. "I don't even remember what I ordered. I've been trying to get him to ask me out for so long that I just sat there in amazement savoring the moment."

Her mom nodded. "True. You've been working on it for a while. So what happened? Did you find anything to talk about?"

"We talked." She grew pensive. "You know, he's five years older than me. Now that we're both out of school, the age difference doesn't seem to matter much. Do you think it should?"

"Not really. I agree with you."

"Mom, he's so nice looking. Parker is handsome, but Gavin is dreamy. Those dark eyes of his look right through me. I'd die for his long thick eyelashes." She sighed.

"Remember, dear, character counts. Beauty fades—always."

Brianne shot back, "I admire his character. But it comes with such black wavy hair." She folded her arms and stared into space.

Her mom tilted her head. "Aren't we getting a little ahead of the game? Are you officially seeing each other?"

"Who knows? I haven't a clue. He was as nervous as the proverbial cat. Hopefully, I'll see him at church tomorrow."

"One step at a time." She poured the batter into a pan and passed the leftovers in the bowl to her daughter.

Malcolm finished putting the last dish in the dishwasher. He wiped down the cabinets, soon to join the Saturday night Bible study in progress in the living room. Once there, he plopped down on a big cushion reserved for latecomers. All the seats were taken—a welcomed sight. As residents completed their supervised release, newbies came in on their heels. Most arrived directly from prison but a few entered straight from drug rehab.

Parker always had more candidates than he could accommodate. He selected those with the greatest chance of success. Malcolm felt sad for those who were turned away. If only they had more beds?

Parker acknowledged his entrance into the room with a nod. "We're just starting the Book of John," he said. After a volunteer read the first five verses, Parker posed the question, "Who is *the Word* mentioned in verse one?"

The discussion continued for the following hour and a half. Then the group adjourned to the carriage house, which Parker had converted into a game room, complete with a pool table, foosball table, and folding tables for card games.

Malcolm watched as Gavin headed out with the guys. He emptied a couple of trashcans from the living room and carried a few stray drinking glasses back to the kitchen. He heard Parker turn on the carpet sweeper to pick up cookie crumbs.

Through the week the residents had assigned and rotating kitchen, housekeeping, and laundry duties, but Saturday was their day off. Malcolm and Parker covered the bases on Saturday.

Everyone was expected to go to church on Sunday with mandatory study time in the afternoon. Every evening consisted of either Bible studies or support group meetings.

Malcolm looked up as Parker came through the kitchen on his way to join the guys in the carriage house. He stopped his boss. "You got any idea what's going on with Gavin?"

Parker furrowed his brow. "No. Is something happening that I need to know about?"

"Probably not. It's just that before dinner he asked me if I'd ever been in love. If so, what did it feel like?"

"Strange. I didn't even know he had a girlfriend. Who is it?"

"He didn't say. Said he was just curious."

"Hmm. And how did you answer his question?" Parker tried to hide a slight grin.

"I had nuthin' for him. Told him to ask Mr. Brooks. He seems happily married."

"Good idea. Well, I'm out with the guys." With that, he ambled through the screen door and headed to the carriage house.

Malcolm furrowed his brow. When did Gavin have time for a girlfriend? He stopped by most every evening on his way home from work. Probably for a square meal.

36

Parker sat at his desk, pencil between his teeth. He surveyed his month-at-a-glance calendar open to the next four weeks. Two men were ending their supervisory probation, and two others were taking their places. Six others remained on the waiting list. All of the residents had steady jobs, a chore list, and Bible study or support groups in the evenings.

He scratched his head. The Sloan House was growing beyond what his staff could provide. Malcolm's duties included transporting men to their probation office appointments and helping them fill out paperwork. He oriented the newbies and held debriefings with those on their way out. He shopped and prepared meals, along with light housekeeping in the common areas.

Malcolm proved absolutely essential to the entire operation. Yet, Parker planned to move him to Miami to open a second halfway house. Who would replace him?

Gavin was already way too involved for his own wellbeing: here practically every day, managing the foundation's legal affairs, and now trying to be active in their church. Plus, Malcolm had hinted that he had a girlfriend. And why hadn't he shared that with him? Gavin did seem to have his head in the clouds. Parker leaned back in his office chair. He'd have to ask him about that.

Then there was Brianne. She still officed at home. The Sloan House had no room to move her into closer quarters. With her brains and talent, how long would she be content to live with her parents? He definitely needed to make it worth her time to stay on. He made a note to substantially increase her salary.

Parker didn't like to think about the wealth he'd inherited. Satan loved to tell him that he was unworthy of Gram Sloan's generosity. He was determined to be a good steward of her money. Brianne and Gavin were the only two people who knew the burdens as well as the blessings of managing a foundation.

His mind wandered back to his days in the Orlando halfway house. How had Conner and Megan managed so capably? Sure, they had Zander, then Parker, then Mitchell, and a host of other guys who'd proven themselves able to handle the kinds of tasks that Malcolm provided him.

An unsettling feeling washed over him. Connor had Megan to help him. She was truly his helpmeet in every definition of the word. Parker had never considered himself marriage material. Gram Sloan had assured him that he'd broken a few hearts in high school, but he'd never noticed. Way too intent on getting out from under his father's control, he'd been laser focused on a career in medicine.

Short of sending for a mail-order bride, he chuckled, he didn't have a clue how to begin finding a mate. Someone with a heart for the disadvantaged. A woman who would share his passion for God's work of transforming lives. He let out a big sigh. A brand new prayer request took shape in his mind.

Meanwhile, maybe God would lead him to a couple to take Malcolm's place.

Brianne sat in the chair across from Parker. They'd finished their weekly team meeting, and Malcolm had headed to the airport to pick up a new arrival.

Brianne again expressed appreciation for her raise. "I'm saving for an apartment of my own, maybe even a two bedroom unit so I can have a real office."

"That would be great," Parker beamed. "Do I detect a willingness to continue working for The Sloan Foundation? At least for the near future?"

She gave him a lopsided grin. "I'm not really looking for another job. Especially now that Gavin and I are dating." At Parker's look of astonishment, she continued. "Well, maybe he doesn't call it dating. Actually, I'm not sure what he calls our time together."

Recovering from his shock, Parker indelicately asked, "So what do you do together?"

Brianne seemed quite nonchalant about the subject. "We spend Saturday mornings together—hiking, working out, swimming, visiting state parks—active stuff. Then he picks me up for church and Bible studies. My friends think of us as a couple. Why, do you know something I don't know?"

Parker shook his head. "No, I didn't know you were seeing each other."

"Strange, huh?" Brianne suggested. "Well, if I'm off base here, will you let me know?" She stood and walked toward the doorway. "I'm enjoying getting to know him. He does keep his cards close to his vest. Fortunately, I love a mystery." She winked and headed through the living room for the front door.

"So why didn't you tell me?" Parker asked. He and Gavin sat on the front porch of the halfway house sipping iced tea. The residents were in their rooms studying on this gloriously sunny Sunday afternoon.

"No reason. We're just hanging out." Gavin looked at his brother, who remained unconvinced. "She's the one who started this. She kept calling me, inviting me to things. What was I supposed to do?"

"Oh, say *no* if you weren't interested?" Parker gloated in uncovering Gavin's secret. "Your dilemma wouldn't have anything to do with her attractive looks and personality, I don't suppose?"

Gavin took a sip of tea. "What if it did? What would you know about dating the opposite sex? Was I supposed to come to you for advice?"

His remark stung. Mostly, because it was absolutely true. He replied evenly, "I only need to know because she's an employee of The Sloan Foundation and so are you—at least you are part-time. Office romances, that sort of thing."

Gavin emptied his glass. "You've got a point. I didn't think of that. I guess you'd call what we do dating. Are we a couple? That term will need to grow on me. Can we drop the subject for now?" When Parker nodded, he asked, "When are we breaking the news to Malcolm about his new assignment? The feasibility study has been sitting on your desk for two weeks."

Parker sighed. "I know. I just can't do without him right now."

Parker surprised Connor with his call. They'd talked on numerous—if not regular—occasions, but this call seemed unexpected. "What can I do for you, pal?" he asked. "Or did you just call to see if my daughter is still the most beautiful female on the planet? Er, next to my wife, that is."

Parker laughed. "If Amber still looks like Megan, I'd say you've got a tie." The men took a few minutes to catch up with each other. Then Parker got down to business.

"I need more help here in Nashville." Connor already knew about the Miami halfway house possibility. In fact, he'd been scouting for an assistant to help Malcolm set up the new facility.

Parker informed him that he'd received a positive feasibility study, and a large house in an older part of Miami had become available. It was time to tell Malcolm and begin the transition.

"I can't let Malcolm go without a replacement here. I believe I'd like to hire a couple. Someone like you and Megan. A team. Committed to the work we do."

"Well, we're one of a kind," Connor bragged with false bravado. "But maybe we can find a second-best couple."

"You do that," Parker grinned. "And fast. I need them here yesterday.

37

Malcolm knew something big was up. Parker had been jumpy the last few days. Brianne was absentminded, and Gavin ducked out of conversations with him whenever possible. Even some of the residents had commented on the change in the atmosphere during their meals.

When Parker finally invited Malcolm to a meeting with the two other staff members, he prepared himself for whatever was coming. Never in a thousand years would he have guessed the topic of conversation. Parker began the meeting with the usual prayer thanking God for His rich blessings and asking for wisdom and guidance.

He turned to Malcolm while Gavin and Brianne looked on. "I've had a dream for a long time now. It's a dream that involves your mother."

Malcolm's eyes grew wide. His mom had been deceased for a number of years. "I know how much you loved her," Parker continued. "In fact, you gave me up as the perfect cellmate to transfer to a prison closer to Miami." He turned to Gavin and Brianne. "She wasn't well enough to travel to central Florida to see him.

"When you were released, you began a street ministry in Miami with young men on the docks who were headed in the same wrong direction that landed you in prison. Your problem was a lack of resources: a funding source and an organization to give you backup."

Malcolm looked around the room. "What is this? The show, 'This is Your Life?' Where are the cameras?"

Parker kept talking. "Then your mother died. You were at a low point when I called and invited you to come to Nashville and help me get this place off the ground."

"Good thing you did," Malcolm interrupted. "I was down to my last doughnut. Are you trying to make me blubber like a baby?" Then his expression turned to alarm. "Am I getting the boot?"

"Sorta," Gavin interrupted. "But it's a better-made boot with more miles left on it."

Brianne jumped in. "Don't tease him. Malcolm, we think we've got very good news for you. Don't we, guys?" She gave them a warning look before settling back in her chair.

"Okay," Parker sighed. "Here goes: how would you like to open your very own halfway house in Miami?"

Malcolm sat very still while his eyes darted back and forth among them. Parker continued, "I know this seems out of the blue, but I've been hoping for this for some time."

"I can vouch for that," Gavin added. "He told me ages ago."

"I would like to call it The Amelia Winton House in honor of your mother," Parker announced. "Of course, The Sloan Foundation would support it. I'll share the other details with you later, but first, are you interested?"

A huge tear inched its way down Malcolm's right cheek. He bowed his head and began to sob, blubbering like a baby.

Two weeks later Malcolm flew to Miami to look over the proposed location of The Winton House. He looked forward to meeting Curt, who'd been recommended by Connor and Megan as his assistant. Once he landed, picked up a rental car, and checked into his hotel, he headed to the cemetery to talk over his good news with Amelia Winton.

He carried a vase filled with a bouquet of artificial flowers and set them at the foot of her grave. "Ma," he began. "How would you like to have a house named for you? We never got to own a home before. This one is real big with lots of windows. I'm going to see it soon and make an offer. You would love the leafy trees and the neighborhood.

"Ma, I'm going to be living there with lots of guys just like me, guys looking for a new way of life with a Savior named Jesus guiding the way. I know I disappointed you, Ma. But I'm going to make you proud. I'm never going to forget that this is your house, too, the house you never got to live in with a son who misses you very much. I love you. Rest in peace."

Slowly, he rose and headed back to the car. He cast a glance back over his shoulder at the vase of flowers, already picturing a flowerbed for a home he had yet to see.

Parker sat in his living room tapping his fingers on the arm of his chair. When the doorbell rang, he rose immediately. A young Latino couple, Ruben and Rosa Alvarez, stood on the porch at The Sloan House. Parker ushered them inside and asked them to take a seat on the couch.

Parker, at six-feet-four inches, felt like a giant looking down at them. Ruben had a lighter complexion than his wife. He spoke without an accent and seemed quite comfortable in the new surroundings. She had big brown eyes and a lovely smile with a row of perfect white teeth. Both had shiny black hair and were dressed appropriately for an interview in slacks and colorful shirts.

The three of them sat in the living room. Rosa looked around with a woman's eye for details. Ruben waited for him to begin. They talked for about an hour before Parker offered to show them around.

Rosa had been fairly quiet during Parker's friendly interrogation, but now she asked numerous questions. Malcolm could have answered them better, but he'd been running errands all afternoon. Now he was headed to pick up a resident from a probation hearing.

Once inside the carriage house, Parker explained the purpose of the game room. "I didn't want the guys looking for a pool hall or watching too much television. This way Malcolm or I can keep them busy while also befriending them."

Upstairs, Rosa looked over Malcolm's living quarters with great interest. The living room was spacious and included a kitchenette. The bedroom had a walk-in closet and a bathroom with tub and shower, double sinks, and a big linen closet. She clasped her hands together and smiled, mixing Spanish and English words back-to-back as Latinos often do when English is a second language.

Parker explained that the living area was big enough to add a second bedroom, but he'd waited to see if one would be needed. The young couple grinned at each other, and Rosa shyly ducked her head.

She asked to stay behind and do some measuring while Ruben and Parker went to the study to talk over the details of employment. It soon became apparent that Ruben had a business head on his shoulders and a fair amount of experience in negotiation.

Malcolm unloaded several sacks of groceries and then joined Parker in his office. They had about an hour before the guys needed to be picked up from work. Malcolm was eager to hear Parker's report on the visit with the couple that might be replacing him.

Parker rattled off the particulars and his observations with the precision of a former surgeon. "Ruben has lived in the U.S. all his life. His parents settled in New York from Spain. He grew up speaking English and has a bachelor's degree in social work from Virginia Tech."

Malcolm jotted a few notes on his pocket notebook. Parker continued, "His first job brought him to Orlando, where he worked with troubled youth. He'd grown up around gangs, addiction, and dysfunctional families, although his own family managed to avoid the problems of urban life. They were church-going Christians who lived their faith. That's why Ruben decided to be a social worker.

"In Orlando he met Rosa. You might say opposites attract." At this Parker grinned. "She was a teenager, an immigrant from Central America, and definitely running with the wrong crowd. In fact, he hinted that she'd had some exposure to sex exploitation.

"To make a long story short, Rosa was rescued by a halfway house for exploited women, became a Christian, and started a Twelve Step program. Having a burning desire to help others caught in the web of the lies and distortions of sex traffickers, she began studying to lead groups through recovery programs.

"They met at a recovery workshop led by—you guessed it—Connor and Megan. The couples became good friends, and the rest is history.

"My observation: Ruben has definitely got the qualifications to lead Bible studies, as well as support groups. Rosa needs a little more seasoning. He says she's a quick study and highly motivated. They seem very likeable and resourceful."

"So do you think you'll hire them?" Malcolm asked.

"The issue may be whether they'll agree to work with me. You'd better give me a glowing recommendation."

"Thinkin' on it." Malcolm grinned and headed toward the kitchen.

38

Parker sat with his fingers steepled together under his chin. The past several months had passed in a whirlwind. Malcolm had settled into The Winton House with Curt as his assistant. Parker looked forward to meeting Curt soon when he made his next trip to the Miami location.

The opening would be attended by three of the Sloan Foundation board members, an official from the Florida Department of Corrections, and local officials in Miami Dade County. Chaplain Jake had recommended two residents who were being released from the central Florida prison where he worked. Parker had emptied his waiting list to fill the other available spaces.

Meanwhile, he oriented Ruben and Rosa to their duties, as well as hiring a fulltime housekeeper. That had been one of Ruben's negotiating successes. Rosa liked having another woman around, and Parker agreed the arrangement avoided any uncomfortable situations.

Rosa turned out to be a fabulous cook—so good that the guys fought to be on the kitchen rotation. She shared her recipes willingly and let them copy the instructions for future use. Ruben alternated leading Bible studies with Gavin and Parker. Ruben handled the support group meetings with a firm hand. Gavin joked that "he takes no prisoners."

Parker asked him if his own compassionate side was a blind spot when he led groups. Gavin quipped, "I don't know. The tissue box you keep by the side table might be a clue."

During the Bible studies Rosa was gifted at keeping the testosterone at acceptable levels. He'd almost forgotten what a helpful addition Megan had made to their evening sessions in Orlando. A woman's perspective and instincts helped the guys develop more precise communication. Most of the men hadn't been around ladies in years and needed to refresh their manners.

In short, the Alvarez addition had been a windfall for The Sloan House. He'd thanked Connor a dozen times. He'd replied, "You keep opening halfway houses, and I'll train the leaders."

Gavin had grown comfortable with the idea that Brianne and he were dating. In the eyes of their church singles group, they were a couple. He couldn't believe his good fortune. Now with the arrival of Ruben and Rosa, he had more time to devote to their blossoming relationship.

On this particular Saturday morning, he and Brianne sat side by side on the bank of the Cumberland River with a fishing pole in their hands. She glanced his way. "Do you even have a worm on your hook?"

"The worm and I talked it over. We decided he needed a day off."

"So how do you plan to catch a fish?"

"You said we were taking a relaxing walk to your dad's favorite fishing spot. You said nothing about actually fishing."

Brianne shook her head. "Next time I'll be more specific. I thought perhaps the fishing poles and can of worms would have tipped you off."

Gavin pulled his ball cap over his eyes and lay back on the grassy riverbank. "While you wait for a bite, what relaxing thoughts are flowing between your cute little ears?"

Brianne leaned back on an elbow to look at him. "Oh, just wondering when I'll get to meet your parents."

Gavin gave a start. She'd found a hot button. "Actually, I had dinner with Dad and Mom last night. They said they were booked up for the next six months."

Brianne ripped his cap off his head and dangled it above him. "I don't believe you."

Gavin sat back up and grabbed his cap. "I can't even get them to invite Parker over."

"Parker's not your girlfriend. Every mother wants to meet the girl her son is dating."

"But you're not from a wealthy family with social standing. You're much too religious." Gavin grew serious. "And you work for Parker."

Brianne's expression turned somber. "I guess that's three strikes."

"I'm sorry. I'm truly sorry. Let's give it some time."

Parker and Ruben were examining the month's financials in his office when the phone rang. Parker recognized Ted Poole's number and picked up the call.

"Hey, Ted. How are you? ... What? ... How did it happen? ..." A long silence ensued. He asked, "What can I do? ... Sure thing. Thanks for letting me know. I be praying."

Slowly Parker put the phone back on the hook. Ruben waited for him to speak. Parker rose from his chair and walked the short distance to his window. He put his head in his hands and began to weep.

Ruben slipped him a tissue from the ever-present box on his desk. Moments later, Parker quieted and bowed his head in prayer.

Ruben's chair squeaked as he stood to leave, but Parker stopped him. "I'll tell you what I heard. I just needed a moment to—"

"I understand," said Ruben. "If you'd rather—"

"No. Please sit back down." Parker took his seat behind the desk, still dabbing at his eyes. "That was our doctor, Ted Poole. You haven't met him yet—which is good. I'm glad you haven't needed his services. He's a great guy and a good friend.

"Ted's the one who asked me to serve as medical director at the clinic off Charlotte Avenue. The receptionist there is a woman named Kathy Collins. Her husband, Roy, a local pastor, was on the planning committee for the clinic and very supportive of the work we did for those unable to pay for services.

"Roy was in his office today when a man looking for cash robbed and stabbed him. His secretary had hidden in a closet. When the man left, she found him and called 911. He died at the hospital."

"Oh, man." Ruben bowed his head.

"He and Kathy have three children. I can't imagine what she's going through." Parker grabbed another tissue. "Ted just wanted our prayers. Her church family is providing everything they need right now. Both of their parents are on the way to Nashville."

"May I lead us?" Ruben asked. Parker nodded. Ruben asked his heavenly Father for comfort for the family. Then he rose and placed a hand on Parker's shoulder. "And for my brother, Parker, whose spirit is wounded right now. Surround him with Your peace, not based on circumstances but on Your holy Presence."

"Thank you." Parker stood and gave his coworker a hug. "Roy was such a good man. I can't believe he's gone."

The following afternoon Ted Poole and Parker Hamilton stood on the porch of the Collins residence. Parker had called ahead to see if their visit would be convenient. He held a platter filled with sandwiches straight from Malcolm's kitchen while Ted carried a chocolate cake baked by his wife Susan.

Kathy opened the door, her daughter Gina clinging to her skirt. She ushered them inside to the family room where her sons David and Matthew were playing with toy cars on the hardwood floor. The men handed their food plates to a friend who'd taken them to the kitchen while another friend was posted by the telephone, pen and paper in hand.

When Kathy sat down, Gina hopped on her lap, thumb in her mouth. David and Matt looked up to say hello and went back to their play. Both men knew the children well—Ted as their family doctor and Parker from their frequent trips with their mom to the clinic. Kathy's tear-streaked face and swollen eyes told them volumes about how she was feeling, but they asked anyway—not sure how else to begin the conversation.

"Honestly, I'm hurting. But so are many others. Roy's secretary, Janet, the one who found him, is not doing well at all. Please pray for her. I still haven't seen his body. The situation is a little surreal, to be frank."

Parker thought back to his days in the medical examiner's office. Bodies involved in a crime often weren't released to the family for days.

"Since it's a police matter, I can't tell you much," Kathy continued. "They caught a man who matched Janet's description. The lab has taken blood samples from his clothing. He's behind bars."

While Ted asked a few more questions, Parker scooted over to where the boys were sitting on the floor. The oldest of the children, ten-year-old David, was quiet and wouldn't make eye contact. Parker surmised that he'd turned inward in a self-protective shell. Matthew, only four years old, remembered Parker from hours spent in the clinic when his mom brought him to work with her.

He was eager to tell Parker about the various cars and which were the fastest. He stopped suddenly and looked intently at Parker. "My Daddy's in heaven now, did you know? Someday, I'm going to heaven, too, and I'll see him again." Matthew smiled and went back to zooming his cars around the floor.

The funeral service for Roy Collins was packed. The media was present since the story had been broadcast nationwide. Roy's childhood preacher gave the sermon, followed by a number of eulogies. Parker had declined to speak, knowing he wouldn't be able to make it through his tears. Ted Poole spoke for them both, giving a moving tribute to their friend.

Life certainly isn't fair, he thought. Roy had a passion for the poor, people struggling to make ends meet. His church had a food pantry and clothing room. It helped support the medical clinic. Roy had planned to offer a Twelve Step program in the fall. If the man who stabbed him would have asked, Roy could have seen that his needs were met. Now he was sitting in a jail cell with a murder charge hanging over his head.

After the graveside service, Parker stood at the end of the line to speak to Kathy. He approached her, not quite sure what he'd say. Kathy reached out her hands to him and spoke first. "I so appreciate your coming. I know how you loved Roy and my kids. David is hurting and Matt is just bewildered. If you could drop by sometime and take them for ice cream or something—I know it's asking a lot—it would mean a great deal to me."

Parker breathed a sigh of relief. Something tangible he could do for her. "I'd be thrilled," he exclaimed. "Thank you for suggesting it."

A couple of weeks later, Parker and David were hitting balls in a local batting cage. Gavin and Matt were watching from the soda fountain in the entrance of the multi-sport facility. They'd already ridden the bumper cars and struck up a conversation around the Transformer toy Matt carried in his pocket.

At the batting cage, David shouted his disappointment at every ball he missed. His anger got hotter as he flailed at each pitch. Finally, he knelt on the base and burst into tears. Parker quickly recognized the tears as far more than exasperation at his batting average. He needed to cry. His tears weren't about missed hits. He cried for a missed father.

Parker let him cry, eventually moving over to place a strong hand on his shoulder. When David's tears dried up, Parker gripped his shoulder. "Let's go get some ice cream." They walked together toward the soda fountain.

Parker and Gavin dropped the boys at the Collins house. Brianne's square-cut car was in the driveway. She'd taken seven-year-old Gina to the mall toy store. When the three of them met back at The Sloan House, they shared their experiences with the children.

Brianne couldn't wait to tell the guys Gina's observations about the various window displays in the mall. "The child has fashion sense," Brianne said. "However, she was far more interested in my prosthesis. She dubbed it a woo-leg—a wooden leg. Isn't that hilarious? Of course, it's not really made of wood, but she wasn't interested in the specifics. She asked me if I knew about Captain Hook, who lost a hand."

Gavin liked the woo-leg moniker and threatened to use it. Brianne caught him in a chokehold. Parker broke up the fight. Then Gavin admitted how hard it had been to keep up with a four-year-old. "And I thought I was a hunk." Brianne rolled her eyes.

Parker shared a request to pray especially for David. "He's having a tough time, both missing his dad and feeling responsible for the others. I just let him talk. Maybe someday we'll have a relationship that will give me permission to offer some thoughts. I was the oldest child in our family. Imagine feeling responsible for Alexis and Gavin."

Brianne glanced at Gavin. "A burden to be sure."

"Well, this *burden* would like to pray for David right now." As they bowed their heads, Gavin asked the Comforter for a special gift of peace for a little lost sheep wandering in a pit filled with grief.

At the three-month anniversary of Roy's death, Parker asked if he might treat the Collins family to a meal at their favorite restaurant. They chose Cracker Barrel, a chain that began in the Nashville area.

The kids ordered fried chicken and tried to figure out the wooden tee-hopping game positioned on each table. Their interest allowed Parker a moment to talk to their mother. He already knew she'd taken a leave of absence from the clinic.

"I'll need a better paying position long term, but for now, Roy's life insurance is our lifeline. Of course, his parents want us to move back to our hometown. I don't want to uproot the children right now. Our church family has been incredible. I need them as much as the kids do for now."

Parker just listened. She didn't need his advice as much as she needed a sounding board. They finished their meal and headed back home. Parker walked them to the door. "Call me anytime," Parker volunteered to Kathy.

"I will. I see all that support group training you've had has really paid off." She grinned and shooed the kids in the door.

40

Gavin pulled his sedan into the circular driveway of his boyhood home. Brianne waited for him to open the car door for her. She gracefully stood up and practically bumped into his chin.

Gavin peered down at her. "Have I told you how beautiful you look this evening?"

"Yes. But I need to hear it again."

"Blue should always be your go-to color. Of course, I also like you in green and red. Did you know redheads can wear red?"

Brianne chuckled at one of her mother's favorite lines. "Are you stalling for time?"

"Yes."

"Well, I'm perfectly ready. Usher me in, sir."

"I'm trying to remember why I brought you here."

"To meet your parents, silly! My dad advised me just to be me. If they don't approve, it's their loss." She tossed her strawberry curls and headed for the front door.

"Sure you wouldn't prefer a burger and fries?" Gavin reached the door just as Louisa, the housekeeper, opened it. Gavin greeted her with a kiss on the cheek as they stepped into the massive foyer.

"Miss Louisa, may I introduce Brianne Brooks."

"Good evening, Miss Brooks. May I take your wrap?"

"Thank you, but I believe I'll keep it." She pulled the drape around the shoulders of her calf-length gown. Glancing around the foyer, she marveled at the winding staircase to the second floor on her left and the large drawing room to her right.

Brianne turned back to Louisa. "I understand you've known Gavin all his life? Perhaps you could share a few stories with me?"

Louisa smiled demurely. "I'm afraid I'm sworn to silence. If you'll follow me, Mr. and Mrs. Hamilton are waiting in the parlor."

Gavin steered his guest by the elbow as they entered a small but tastefully decorated living area. The Hamiltons were seated on the sofa and rose to meet them.

Brianne almost gasped at his lovely mother, dressed in white linen with matching heels. With her blonde shoulder-length hair and high cheekbones, she looked more like a runway model than a mother of three young adults. Her coloring matched that of Parker, who'd often claimed to look more like the Sloan branch of the family tree.

Mr. Hamilton was obviously the source of Gavin's dark hair and eyes. He stepped forward and extended his hand. Brianne noted the firm grasp, followed by a limp response from his mother. "Just call me Olivia. And my husband is Hollister."

She invited the young couple to sit in side chairs facing the sofa. After a few pleasantries, the grilling began. Her family background; her schooling; future job prospects. Gavin allowed the questioning to run its course before he interrupted.

"Brianne asked me if she could explain the circumstances around her lost limb." The Hamiltons glanced at each other uncomfortably. Obviously, they weren't planning to bring up the subject. Gavin continued, "The story plays an important role in who she's become, and she's pleased to tell it."

Olivia recovered first and assured her they'd be glad to hear it, although she owed them no explanation.

"It's my delight to tell you," Brianne began. "I call my leg my trophy of God's grace." She recounted the story of how her first cancer at age four had brought her parents back together after their divorce. Then a second bout of cancer at age nine had cost her an amputation below her left knee.

Weaving through her story were glimpses of how God had been at work through her Meme and Papa Dyer, Pastor Frank and Mrs. Myra, and the many friends who had prayed for her. Olivia sat through the retelling with little facial expression. However, Hollister grew more impatient as she talked. He was obviously relieved when Louisa appeared at the door to announce dinner would be served in the dining room.

He escorted Brianne to the formal dining room while Gavin offered his arm to his mother. Her stage whisper could easily be heard by all. "You look smashing, darling. You must come by more often."

Gavin parked his car in front of Brianne's home. He let out a big sigh. Brianne looked at him from the passenger's seat. "Was that a sigh of relief, or discouragement, or simple exhaustion?"

"Yes," he replied. "Sorry to put you through that. But at least you can no longer say you haven't met my parents."

"That wasn't so bad. Not compared to my root canal."

Gavin raised an eyebrow. "Or my soccer concussion."

"At least we accomplished mission number one. I shared my Christian testimony with a captive audience."

Gavin turned to face her. "We did pull that off, didn't we? I'm so glad they heard your story. A seed was planted. That's what we are. We're seed planters."

"You got that right." Brianne settled back against the seat cushion. "What do you suppose they're saying about me?"

"Oh, a beautiful woman, great personality, obviously intelligent, seemed to think our son is a genius."

Brianne couldn't help but laugh. Gavin pulled her toward him. "If not, I'd say they're a poor judge of character."

Monday morning Parker picked up the ringing telephone and shouted his hello to Malcolm. "How's it going, buddy?" The men talked business for a few minutes. Parker reviewed the details of his upcoming trip to Miami the following week. "I'm eager to see how you've spruced up the place. I hope you've taught Curt how to cook."

The bantering continued until Malcolm asked for a progress report on Gavin's love life. "You know, he asked me if I'd ever been in love."

"He's a goner," his brother exclaimed. "The guy can't keep a straight thought in his head. It's a wonder he still has a job. Brianne's getting her work done, or I'd fire her for hanging out with a space cadet."

Malcolm laughed, then asked if there was anything he could pray for him about. "Hmm," Parker thought. "Prayer request? Gavin thinks that now that he's broken the ice with Brianne coming over to meet our parents, he can get an invitation for me. I hope so. It may take an act of God."

A couple of weeks later Parker stood at the front door of the Hamilton's Belle Meade residence. He couldn't decide whether to ring the doorbell or walk on in. After all, he grew up in this house. Shouldn't he act like he was home?

Gavin saved him the trouble of deciding. He opened the door just as Parker was about to knock. "Come on in," he invited.

Louisa stood behind him. She smiled at him with obvious pleasure. Parker smiled back and kissed her on the cheek. "Good to see you. I dressed for dinner, thanks to your constant reminders."

She grinned and left to announce his arrival. Gavin ushered him into the kitchen, where he greeted Clarissa, the cook, with a big hug.

"Young man, you're going to get tomato sauce all over your nice suit. ... Oh, put me down. ... Master Parker, it's so good to see you."

Parker toured the kitchen, lifting lids and opening the oven. He asked about the other household employees he'd gotten to know on his way to and from the houses on their cul-de-sac while growing up.

Then Gavin led him to their father's study, where his parents were awaiting his arrival. Parker straightened his hair and suit coat. *Only by the grace of God ...* he reminded himself as he walked through the door.

His mother sat in a chair facing the desk where his father labored over a document lying in front of him. She had a drink in one hand and gazed out the window at the manicured lawn.

When Parker entered the room, she rose and gave him a two-cheek kiss before returning to her seat. His father looked up and mumbled a hello before leaning back in his leather chair. His two sons squeezed onto a small settee. Gavin broke the ice by talking about the legal paper lying on the desk. Eventually, small talk ended, and an uncomfortable silence enveloped the room.

Parker spoke up. "Thank you for inviting me to dinner."

"Gavin invited you," his father corrected. "We agreed to eat here at the same time."

Parker felt the familiar gut punch to his abdomen.

"Oh, Hollister," his mother implored, "can't we enjoy a simple family dinner?" She rose and took Parker's elbow. "Let me show you how we've redecorated the dining room now that you youngsters aren't dropping food all over the floor."

Gavin fell in behind them and began whistling a popular tune. Parker would never have been allowed to whistle in the house. Maybe a small amount of jealousy lingered between his brother and him.

Sitting in The Sloan House living room, legs sprawled in front of him, Gavin popped M&Ms into his mouth. Parker cracked his knuckles, attention seemingly in another place. Ruben and Rosie were in the game room in the former carriage house, supervising the men.

Parker spoke. "At least Mother asked about The Sloan House. I almost felt a little pride from her, since the foundation is named after her mother, Abigail Sloan."

Gavin finished his mouthful of chocolate candy. "Only that reminded Dad of losing the lawsuit against you for the money in her will. His eyebrows were pasted together for the rest of the evening."

"One parent at a time, I guess. At least I felt a little warmth from Mother. And since when do you call our father *Dad*?"

"Whenever I want. You take him far too seriously. He's not the tough man you think he is."

Parker frowned. *Could've fooled me.*

41

An outing with a member of the Collins family became a regular feature of Parker's life. Occasionally, he accompanied David to a sports or scout's event that his dad would have eagerly taken him to. Still, David maintained his distance as though to remind Parker that he wasn't his father. Parker respected the boy's need to make sure Roy wasn't forgotten.

On the other hand, Matt and Gina danced at the window when they saw his car pull up in the driveway. Matt seemed to always have a different toy he wanted to show him. Gina would cling to his leg until he picked her up in his arms.

According to Kathy, Gina cried when he left them at the door. He wasn't sure what to do about her growing dependency on him. Kathy didn't seem concerned, but it definitely bothered him. In one of Gina's run-on commentaries, she'd unconsciously called him dad.

Kathy had returned to work at the clinic. For her own mental health, she'd said. The trial date for Roy's killer had been set. Sitting at home while the kids were in school and Matt had begun kindergarten left her with jittery nerves and depressive thoughts. She thought it best to keep busy.

One afternoon when Parker brought all three children home from an animated movie, Kathy invited him in to the foyer. Each of them told their favorite part of the story. Then they headed to the family room for the snacks Kathy had left them on the coffee table. Parker had been warned not to purchase salty popcorn or sugary drinks.

Once the kids were out of ear range, Parker said, "Kathy, I'd like to share some observations with you about the children." She immediately stepped out on the porch, Parker behind her, and shut the storm door. "Would you mind if we had this conversation later? I don't want any of them to overhear—"

"No, of course not." He thought quickly. "How about I take you to lunch someplace near the clinic? I'm on the board of directors now, and we do need to talk about your long-range plans." Kathy nodded. They arranged a time and place and wished each other a good evening.

When Kathy arrived out of breath, Parker was already seated at a mom and pop restaurant right on Charlotte Avenue. "Sorry," she lamented. "I needed to wait until Mrs. Jackson retrieved her preschoolers from the waiting area. Since you're on the board, don't you think the clinic could hire a fulltime babysitter?"

"Oh, I remember the days," he reminisced. "In fact, didn't I change Matt Collins' diapers a few times?"

Kathy laughed. "He might have come to work with me when I was nursing him." Her expression became sober. "Many of these mothers have no trustworthy adult to watch their children when they come for a checkup. The oldest child is put in the role of watching the younger ones."

"Which is one of the reasons we opened the clinic. Where else can you get a physical plus good babysitting?" She grinned and agreed with him.

The server came for their orders. Kathy sat back in the booth and focused on the ceiling. "I don't know how long I'll be able to work at the clinic. I need more income." She lowered her hazel eyes to meet Parker's. "But right now, I'm in no condition to job hunt. Until this trial is over, I'm just a complete wreck."

Parker's natural gift of compassion kicked in, and he forgot all about his agenda for their meeting. "I get that," he stated. "Please don't feel any pressure from the board."

"I'm so glad I won't be called to testify, since I wasn't a witness to the crime." She grimaced at the word. "But I will when—not if—he's convicted in the sentencing phase of the trial." She dropped her head into her hands. "How can I even begin to tell the jury the effect Roy's death has had on our family?" Tears began to form in her eyes..

If Parker had nothing else to offer, at least he always carried tissues. He handed a folded stack from his pocket to the distraught widow. He felt the Spirit's tugging. Kathy needed to unburden her heart to someone outside her family and church family. Someone who wouldn't judge her feelings. That's one skill he'd learned by practicing the art of listening.

Parker remained in a somber mood throughout the afternoon. Later Gavin dropped by for a quick bite before his scheduled meeting with Beryl. Parker invited him to eat in his office so they could talk.

"You know everyone in the prosecutor's office," he began. "Tell me about the one assigned to the Roy Collins' murder trial. Is he good?" Parker knew Gavin's specialty was real estate law, but word got around.

"*She* is very good. Plus, the defense has a very weak case. The best they can hope for is something less than a life sentence."

Parker pursed his lips. "I'm glad to know that. But I'll still pray as hard as the persistent widow in Luke 18:2–8."

"Brianne and I pray about the whole situation a lot." He took his last bite of dinner. "I need to go meet Beryl."

Parker rose from behind his desk. "How is Brianne? I don't see her much anymore." His eyes twinkled with mischief. "And how does it feel to be in love?"

Gavin gathered his plate and utensils. "Is that what this is? I'd rather have the flu. At least you get over that." Parker placed his arm around his younger brother's shoulder as they headed for the kitchen.

Brianne limped into the kitchen where her mom had begun dinner preparations. She was testing her newest—and possibly last—prosthesis for some time to come. She had definitely quit growing. At least, that was a blessing. But couldn't her Creator have added a few more inches to her height?

"What's for dinner?" she asked. Just then her dad entered from the garage. He shouted across the living room on his way to join them, "What's for dinner?"

The cook frowned at her husband. She pointed to the stove. "How do you even know this is for you?"

He took her in his arms and began swinging her around the kitchen island to an off-key tune. "Because you love me," he whispered. "There's absolutely no other explanation."

Brianne stood by the refrigerator and watched as the couple moved to a slow waltz. Her dreamy gaze expressed the wishes of her own heart. Someday she'd dance with her own true love.

42

Gavin and Brianne sat on beach towels on the grassy slope of the outdoor pool at his dad's club. Tired of swimming, they enjoyed the warmth of an early summer day. Brianne claimed she was tanning, but with her light complexion, he knew the sun would only turn her skin a shade of red. He'd promised to help her watch for the telltale signs of a sunburn.

She handed him a bottle of suntan lotion and turned her back to him. While he lathered her neck and shoulders, she complained that he only had to look toward the sun to turn a fashionable brown. She put her lotion into her tote, then reattached the prosthesis to her left leg. She hadn't needed it to glide through the water.

"Does it still bother you?" he asked.

"What?" She turned her head toward him. "Oh, the new woo-leg?" she asked, using the name the Collins kids had given it. "A little. I'm used to the process, so it doesn't bother me as much as it bothers you."

He was bothered by anything that caused her pain or discomfort. Compassion for others had never before been his strong suit. For some reason, Parker had seemed to be born with a caring heart. Now Gavin's was definitely an outgrowth of his love for his Lord. But even that didn't completely explain why he felt so protective toward Brianne, so concerned for her wellbeing and happiness.

She grabbed a clean towel from her tote and began drying her hair. He was mesmerized watching her. She seemed to have no clue as to her physical beauty. Yet, it wasn't her outward beauty that drew him to her.

He'd dated many beautiful women, but none compared with this woman whose inside was as comely as the outside.

It occurred to him that he'd never voiced his true feelings for her. At first, their relationship had majored on friendship and camaraderie, snappy comebacks, and spiritual growth. It had definitely deepened. Brianne meant more to him than a dating relationship. He had an unfamiliar urge to tell her so.

She had finished toweling her hair and asked for his help to stand. He held out his arms and casually pulled her into an embrace. "Let's go somewhere romantic tonight for dinner. Wear something special."

"What's the occasion?" she asked.

"It's National Date the Most Beautiful Woman in the World Day. Check it out on the calendar." He kissed her, their lips interlocking several times before he let loose of her waist.

"I sure hope that's me," she sighed.

"Obviously." Then he kissed her again.

Gavin had to pull some strings to get a Saturday night reservation at one of Nashville's finest restaurants. The maître d' seated them at a corner booth in one of the more private areas. After they ordered, Gavin took both her hands in his and gazed at her with a silly grin on his face. She tipped her head, a puzzled look on her face.

"I'm wondering why we haven't done this before," he said. "I'm a casual guy, but really, I'm ashamed I haven't treated you to a fancy dinner before. You deserve much better."

Brianne reached over and put her hand on his forehead. "Normal temperature." She reached for his wrist. "Let me check your pulse."

"I'm serious. Hey, while we wait for our meal, let's dance." He led her to the dance floor and began a slow swaying move, getting adjusted to leading a lady with a disability. After a couple of songs, they were moving in sync, singing along to the songs' lyrics.

Their meals arrived and they both ate with relish. Neither said much, but the silence seemed comfortable. The after dinner coffee arrived and Gavin sensed that the time had come.

"Brianne, I have something to tell you. But I don't want you to think you have to say the words back to me. I've felt this way for a long time, but it's taken awhile for me to say it out loud."

She appeared to stop breathing. He rushed on, "I want to tell you that ... that I love you."

She let out a big breath. Immediately, her eyes began to glisten. A beautiful smile spread across her face. "Oh, Gavin, I've loved you for ever so long! This is one of the happiest days of my life." She leaned across the table and gave him a sweet, tender kiss.

Brianne waltzed into her living room from the front porch. Both parents were sitting on the couch watching a television sitcom. They looked up, then looked at each other. "What's up?" her dad said.

"You look very happy," her mom added. "That must have been a delicious meal."

"Forget the food," Brianne squealed. "I'm in love, I'm in love, I'm in love—" she sang from an old Rodgers and Hammerstein song—"I'm in love with a wonderful guy."

Her dad stood up and took her in his arms. "I sure hope that's Gavin, or he's going to be one disappointed guy."

Parker knew Gavin had cancelled their usual Saturday game night for a date with Brianne. As a result, he was surprised when Gavin stopped by The Sloan House after he took Brianne home. He sure hadn't expected to see him in a nice suit and tie.

Gavin sat down in the chair nearest Parker. Everyone else was involved in some form of entertainment. Parker asked, "What's with the fancy duds?"

"I'm in love." Gavin stared into space.

Parker shot a glance at his profile. Since he'd been with Brianne, the object of his affection seemed obvious. Nevertheless, he played along. "I'm assuming Brianne is the lucky woman."

"And she loves me."

"Congratulations." He waved his hand in front of Gavin's face to get his attention. Gavin turned bewildered eyes in his direction.

"Do you want to tell me about it?" Parker scooted his chair closer for privacy.

"Can you believe it? She loves me too."

"I got that part. Maybe you could tell me the part that led up to 'she loves me.'"

Later that evening, after Gavin had floated on air to his car, Parker tried to piece his story into a coherent flow. Something about how Gavin didn't deserve her, but neither did her father. That statement made absolutely no sense.

If he hadn't known his brother was sober, he'd have made him a strong cup of coffee.

43

Parker sat slumped over the spreadsheet on his desk. There had to be a way to accommodate more men in his halfway house. The only space he could add—and remain in compliance with the neighborhood covenants—would be to convert his large bedroom and walk-in closet into two rooms, adding space for four new residents. His bath could be turned into a second hall bath.

That would require his moving to another location. Was he ready to give up the close access to the men, as well as direct supervision of Ruben and Rosie? He jotted numbers on the spreadsheet.

Mentally, he weighed the pros and cons. Ruben and Rosie were completely trustworthy in terms of day-to-day management of The Sloan House. The housekeeper had made their workload more manageable. They were presently training a fine young man to assume the role Zander and he had played in the Orlando halfway house, which served as his model.

His long-term goal was to open numerous halfway houses across the nation. He reminded himself that he wouldn't have daily interaction with those residents either. He needed to assume a more administrative and fundraising role instead of hands-on management of one house.

The need was so great for Christian facilities to welcome those seeking to make the huge leap of faith from prison or rehab into mainstream society. The Winton House in Miami stayed full with a waiting list just like The Sloan House.

In addition, he found himself flying to Washington, D.C., to engage members of Congress in proposed legislation regarding prison reform and drug rehabilitation. He could foresee a permanent lobbying effort located somewhere in the capital city. The future of The Sloan Foundation made his head swim.

The cons? Giving up his comfort zone. Turning loose of the place he loved in order to venture into the unknown. Once again, he bowed his head, seeking divine guidance.

Parker dropped David Collins at the front door of his home. His mother opened the door to let him in and walked Parker to his car. Parker told her, "I've got to run, but I enjoyed the outing with David. I'll pick up Gina and Matt Tuesday afternoon after school."

Kathy stood with her arms atop his open car door. "Where are you off to in such a hurry?"

"I'm meeting my realtor at a house for sale on the east side."

"So, you're serious about moving out of The Sloan House?"

"Still thinking about it. I decided looking at some houses might help me decide. I don't know what I'm looking for, so it will be hard to know when I've found it."

"Oh, I love older homes with a history. Checking them out would be my dream job."

Parker's ears perked up. "Would you be willing to go with me to look sometime? I sure could use another set of eyes."

Kathy immediately agreed to help with the hunt. Parker suggested that he ask Brianne when she could sit with the kids. As he drove away, Parker felt an immense sense of relief.

Two days later Parker and Kathy pulled up to a large brick home in the middle of a transitioning neighborhood on Nashville's east side. His realtor had left it unlocked and would be back to close up when they were finished looking.

The house needed lots of love. Sagging shutters with peeling paint greeting them from the front windows. The yard had grown up into a haven for weeds and wildflowers.

A broken sidewalk led to a massive oak front door, its beauty still intact from the early 1900s. Inside, a two-story foyer displayed a carved staircase to the upper floor. A spooky paneled hallway beside the staircase opened to a bedroom and bath.

On the right of the front door a formal living room could easily be turned into an office. On the left a family room with a fireplace led to a dining room and kitchen.

Kathy gave a running commentary on each of the house's features. Parker felt perfectly lost as she mentioned first one thing and then another that could be done to bring it up-to-date. "Whoa," he chided, "all I can hear is 'cha-ching, cha-ching.'"

"Yes," she countered, "but that's assumed in the modest asking price. You'd never find a gem like this for less money."

Parker looked around at the faded carpet and weathered wallpaper. "I'm looking for the gem. Where is it?"

"Where's your imagination?" she teased. As she moved from room to room Parker surmised that if she'd had a tape measure, she'd for sure be measuring for curtains. She climbed the staircase to the second floor, where three bedrooms and a hall bath opened off of a multi-purpose landing.

"What would I do with all this space?" Parker marveled.

"Hmm," Kathy mused. "Fill it with more residents when it's remodeled?"

Parker pursed his lips. The house would be useful for fundraising events and hosting out-of-town guests. It had a ready-made office area and a downstairs bedroom and bath. Back at the front door, Parker scanned the space. "Where would I start?"

"Just with the downstairs for now, and just the rooms you'd need. Transform the bedroom and bath into a master suite with your present furniture. Buy new appliances for the kitchen. A chair and a TV tray and just like that"—she snapped her fingers—"you could move in."

Parker had never lived with such sparse furnishings. Was he ready to move forward with such a major decision?

Three months later, Parker stared at the stack of boxes to be filled from his present office. Not only was he soon giving up his upstairs bedroom but now his office would be Ruben's after he moved out. That decision had come on the heels of Ruben's announcement that the carriage house would soon need that second bedroom Parker had envisioned at first.

Ruben had popped his head into Parker's office a month ago. "Got a minute?" he'd asked. Parker invited him in and waited as the young man sat in the chair across from the desk. Ruben looked at his feet while his light brown skin turned a shade of red. "My wife is in a family way," he announced.

Parker took a moment to interpret the archaic reference to pregnancy. "Congratulations," he said as he extended his right hand. "I'm happy for you both."

"I guess we'll be needing that second bedroom upstairs in our living quarters." He sheepishly added, "And I'll need a place to do my work."

Parker cringed. Of course, Ruben would need an office, just as he'd needed this space. He had planned to office out of his new property, but he now realized the move needed to take place sooner than later. Work had just begun on the old house in east Nashville.

Parker rubbed the back of his neck with his fingers. His mind began to whirl. The company converting his bedroom and bath upstairs was the same one working on his older home. They could easily add the bedroom extension in the carriage house to their contract.

Meanwhile, he hadn't planned to begin the renovation of his newly purchased home with a study/office space. As he thought about it, the room would be easy to remodel. All it needed was a coat of paint and new flooring. And furniture. He made a mental note to call Amy Brooks.

"Tell you what," Parker said to Ruben. "I have an empty office in the house I'm renovating. Give me time to get the necessary changes, electrical hookups, and Internet going over there, and I'll give you my office here." Ruben expressed his gratitude, assuring Parker that he could make do until Parker was ready to move out.

Now Parker stood looking at the empty boxes and the clutter of what would go and stay. Transitions. Life seemed full of them.

44

Parker got off the phone and stood to stretch his long legs. He glanced out the front window as a construction van pulled into his driveway at the older home. More hammering and sawing. His ears were still ringing from yesterday's sounds. The men were hard at work converting the bedroom and bath into a modern master suite. Why had he agreed to move his office to his new address before the downstairs renovation was completed?

He glanced at his watch. Amy Brooks would soon be arriving along with his office furniture. He wandered into the kitchen, where brand new appliances made quite a contrast with the Formica countertops and linoleum flooring. He plugged in the coffee maker and had cups ready when Amy showed up.

They sat on folding chairs as she spread pictures of fabric and paint swatches on the floor in front of him. Before The Sloan House opened, Amy had taken on the job of decorating the structure for its repurposing as a halfway house. She already knew a lot about his tastes in colors and design. However, he felt much less certain about what to do with a house he might live in for the rest of his life. Especially when he might as well be starting from scratch with all the furnishings.

After selecting some choices and eliminating others, Parker asked if Amy might leave the ones he liked with him. "I don't want to make a quick decision I might regret later."

She agreed with his reasoning. "Just give me a call when you're ready to move forward."

Parker asked, "How are things going at your house? I understand Brianne is moving out on her own next week."

"She's already packing. Apartments in Nashville don't come cheap. And she chose the neighborhood very carefully."

Parker dared to ask, "How do you and Layton feel about her move?"

"All little birdies must someday leave the nest. I think the hardest part of parenting is knowing when you've been successful. She needs to fly away and build her own nest."

Just then a furniture delivery truck parked behind the construction van. Amy and Parker walked to the front door. "My lovesick brother may have something to say about how long she lives there alone."

Amy smiled. "Brianne is so happy. She and Gavin make a sweet and handsome couple."

"And how do you and Layton feel?"

"We're very happy too."

Gavin and Brianne leaned back on the grassy bank of the Cumberland River. People were beginning to fill in the few green spots left before the concert began at Riverfront Park. Gavin studied the blue jeaned figure beside him. What was it about her that drew him to her?

He knew beneath one denim leg was a prosthesis. He'd seen it numerous times when Brianne had on shorts or a swimsuit. Somehow, it didn't matter to anyone who knew her, and it certainly didn't to Brianne. He reflected on how her childhood cancer had been a blessing in disguise. Her first bout with cancer had brought her parents back together after their divorce. It proved that her grandmother Meme Dyer was right when she'd said, "God's up to something." The second cancer diagnosis at age nine had cost her dearly: her left leg below the knee. Her *trophy of grace,* she called it.

When he'd asked her what she meant, she'd explained, "I'll probably never know *why* I lost part of my leg, but I've learned to ask *what,* instead. What might my story mean to someone else? My lost limb gives me lots of opportunities to witness to my faith."

Gavin couldn't argue with that. Brianne had been a constant witness to him of God's goodness. He'd learned to love Jesus, and now he loved the young woman who'd nurtured his faith. How he'd grown under her watchful and sometimes take-charge ways! He grinned as he thought of her spunk. Just what he'd had needed to capture his heart.

Gavin reached for one of her strawberry blonde curls, catching her off-guard. In mock horror, she pushed him away, laughing as he toppled onto the grass.

Upright again, Gavin caught her and held her tightly. In days she'd be moving into her own space. Her apartment would give her an actual office to work from. And, as her father had pointed out, the Brooks family would have another guest room.

Would she be content with her job at The Sloan House indefinitely or take another job that might seem more challenging? The Sloan House had become his second home. He loved the prospect of seeing her there when their paths crossed.

Of course, he hoped their paths would cross more often soon. The weekly dates, church activities, and chance meetings at her workplace simply weren't enough contact for his growing attachment to her. Any feelings of self-sufficiency were dissipating quickly. He wanted her by his side, doing life together.

"Do you think your dad will be awake when I get you home tonight?"

"Of course not. Dad will be asleep on the couch as usual. But he'll sit up when he hears my key in the lock and pretend to be reading the paper."

"I have a question I want to ask him."

"Oh, really?" Brianne studied her nails with an impish grin.

"It's about my future plans," he teased.

Brianne poked him in the ribs. "Our future plans, you mean." Gently, she brushed his lips with a kiss as music began to fill the night sky.

News of Gavin and Brianne's engagement spread quickly, although no one was caught by surprise. Her first phone call was to Lori Mays Burton, Brianne's college roommate. She squealed with delight.

Lori had been kept aware of the budding romance for months. Now married for two years, she was soon to deliver her first child, a daughter she hoped to name Brooke, in honor of Brianne's family. Of course, she wanted to know every detail of the engagement.

Brianne recounted the event in her usual detailed way. "When Gavin asked me to wait in his car while he went inside to talk to my dad, I knew the question he would ask him." Lori could hear her chuckle at the other end of the line..

"When he returned to the car with a mischievous grin on his face, I was sure my dad had said *yes*."

"Of course, he would," Lori exclaimed. "They love Gavin—and Parker, too."

Brianne continued, "He helped me out of the car and led me to the backyard porch swing. I was surprised he even knew we had a porch swing. I think *someone* must have clued him in."

"Wonder who?" Lori giggled. "Was your mom awake?"

"She was when we came back inside. But I'm getting ahead of myself." Brianne paused for dramatic effect. "Gavin did the traditional thing—you know—on one knee. What he said was *very* romantic."

Lori smiled as she imagined the scene.

"Then, he pulled a small wrapped object out of his pocket and presented it to me. When I unwrapped it, I saw the most gorgeous diamond I could imagine. I started to protest the cost, but he stopped me. 'Early wedding present from Parker,' he explained. 'It belonged to our Gram Sloan. It was part of the estate he inherited.'"

"Why didn't Parker save it for his future bride?" Lori asked.

"Apparently, Parker didn't think he'd ever need it."

Brianne let out a sigh. "I think he'd make the most wonderful husband. However, I'm the lucky future bride wearing the ring. I'll send you a picture."

"I expect to be invited to the wedding," Lori announced.

"Why, you'll be the matron of honor," she exclaimed. "That is, if you'll go ahead and deliver my namesake child."

"I'm doing all I can," Lori exclaimed. "The rest is up to our Creator." The pair talked on about baby things, as Brianne held out her ring finger, admiring its brilliance.

45

Parker paced back and forth across the faded living room carpet. Tired of trying to make the decisions alone, he'd asked Kathy Collins to stop by on her way to the medical clinic. She'd said she loved older homes and seemed to have definite ideas when they'd first walked into the place.

When he heard the doorbell, he opened the sturdy oak door to find her gazing at the flowerbeds. "Have you hired a landscaper yet?" she asked, without even a hello in his direction. "I think some boxwood shrubs along the front windows would look nice."

She walked back down the front steps. "Since the garage is at the back of the house, a curved driveway would break up the front yard and give you easier access in and out."

Parker grinned at her enthusiasm. "Hi, Kathy. Nice to see you again."

She blushed. "Sorry. Roy and I bought our house before the children were born. I guess I've longed for a new project since he died. I didn't mean to come in and take over."

Parker invited her inside. "Actually, I'd be very glad to have you take over," he admitted. "I'm no good at this."

Kathy peeked through the open French doors into the renovated office. The new carpet and paint complimented the mahogany desk and bookcases. Two upholstered side chairs separated by a round table faced the desk. Shutters flanked the front and side windows.

She turned toward the living room. She stopped and picked at the corner of the faded carpet. When she peeled back the carpet, she whooped at the discovery of the original hardwood floor underneath. Parker stood watching her wipe away the dust and debris covering the wood. "Looks like we've decided what to do about the flooring," he chuckled. "Now I've got fabric and paint swatches and furniture catalogues to show you."

Kathy was late to work that morning. But Parker felt relief and excitement that he'd found a comrade in turning the old house into a lovely home.

Parker sat through the entire Roy Collins murder trial. The jury had returned a unanimous verdict convicting his killer of first-degree murder. Sentencing would begin in two months. Kathy told Parker she had a better feeling of what she would say when she gave her victim impact statement. Still, she dreaded rehashing the trauma her family had endured.

She and the children had gone through the stages of grief and back around more than once. David still had his bouts of anger. Gina remained clingy and insecure. Matt had finished kindergarten and seemed the best adjusted of the three.

Kathy made sure the children talked about their father. She often brought out the family photo albums and videos. No one would forget his lifelong impact on family and friends.

Parker observed the family's grief journey and gained increasing admiration for Kathy's role as surviving parent. He assured her he'd be around to help out as long as she felt she needed his involvement.

Meanwhile, her help with the house renovation more than repaid any of his efforts to befriend her children. She proved to be easy to work with. Best of all, when it came to decisions he had absolutely no clue about, she comfortably took the lead. She laughingly called his house her free therapy.

Days before the final move in date, Parker invited Gavin and Brianne to tour the almost finished project. Although Brianne's mother had assisted with the early design elements and the plans for staging the furniture, she'd been sworn to secrecy about the contents of what she called "the lovely old lady" off Shelby Avenue.

Brianne oohed and aahed over each room of the downstairs. The upstairs would remain as it was for now. Parker was still unsettled about having residents in his private home. That decision could wait.

Brianne claimed she could isolate which design features her mother had suggested. "I know her preferences like the back of my hand," she boasted. "Remember, I played in her office when I was still surrounded by dolls and stuffed animals."

Gavin had watched the transformation of the outside of the structure. Being in real estate law, he knew Parker's new address and had driven by on many occasions "just to see how things were coming along." The lush green lawn was now separated by a curved drive, similar to the one at the Hamilton estate, except for the covered portico at his parents' front entrance.

Window boxes would soon have a variety of flowers. The shrubs and spindly trees would someday reach their desired height. The freshly painted trim and new roof perfectly set apart the polished oak door. Gavin said he was impressed. He slapped him on the back. "Good job, bro."

With their wedding only weeks away, the couple had begun their own house hunting. Brianne would move into Gavin's condo until they found a suitable place to call home. Parker had invited out-of-town guests to a catered pre-wedding gathering at his new place. Alexis planned to fly in from Italy, Brianne's Uncle Kyle from Brussels, and Meme and Papa Dyer from Miami. The occasion might be the only opportunity to show his own parents his refurbished house.

After they left, Parker sat on the bottom step of the staircase looking out the transom window. He felt totally exhausted, as though he'd driven every nail into the new features of this dwelling. The thought of living here alone caught him off guard. He'd lived with the noise of guys down the hallway for years now. He'd still stop by for some of Rosa's cooking.

The new house smell would be a present reminder that he'd entered another new adventure with Christ as His guide. He silently quoted his life verse, first suggested by Chaplain Jake and then quoted by Zander on his first full day at the halfway house: "May our Lord Jesus Christ Himself and God our Father, who has loved us and given us eternal encouragement and good hope by grace, encourage your hearts and strengthen you in every good work and word" (2 Thessalonians 2:16–17).

EPILOGUE

The moving van had been gone for two hours. Parker sat on his new loveseat in the living room, testing to see if he'd made a good choice. Amy Brooks had supervised placing the furniture as the moving personnel brought in each item.

Afterward, Kathy Collins and her children dropped by with staples for his pantry. What would he do with flour, sugar, and spices? Home cooking wasn't one of his specialties. He might have to ask Rosa to share some of her simpler recipes.

He'd enjoyed seeing David, Gina, and Matt again. The last few weeks had been so rushed, he'd not been able to take them on outings. Kathy had insisted on putting away his kitchen items while her children enjoyed watching his big screen television.

Meanwhile, he'd unpacked his suitcase and put the items away in various chests and drawers. His clothes hung neatly in the walk-in closet. Even his toothbrush had a spot near his sink. If only everything would stay where it belonged for at least the first week!

Soon Gavin and Brianne were bringing dinner for the three of them to enjoy. Tentatively, he hoisted his feet onto the coffee table, grinning because no one was there to tell him not to. He leaned back against the soft couch cushion and surveyed the space. His eyes drifted to the dining room. A crystal vase sitting on the long table held the flowers his mother had sent as a welcome gift. On the wall hung a portrait of a young Abigail Sloan atop a beautiful gray mare standing on Kentucky bluegrass.

His thoughts turned to the day he'd received word that Gram Sloan had left him a fortune in her will. He believed she would be very proud of his new home, not to mention the work she had endowed, as well as all that lay ahead.

Tears inched their way down his cheeks. *She loved me for my sake and not for what I could do for her. Kind of like Christ dying for us while we were still sinners.* Gram had instilled in him from an early age Jesus' story of the tiny mustard seed. Whenever he doubted all that God could yet do, she'd taught him to say, *All I need is a little stash of faith in God and in me.*

READER'S GUIDE

Use these questions for personal reflection or group study:

1. What role did Gram Sloan play in Parker's early life?
2. Explain the motto she taught Parker that led to the title of this book.
3. Relate the series of events that led to Parker's drug use.
4. What role did each of the following men play in Parker's salvation story?
   1) Malcolm
   2) Chaplain Jake
5. Did Parker's prison life become easier once he became a Christian? Explain.
6. Ike had strong religious opinions. Why did his beliefs not keep him from prison or drug use?
7. Why did Chaplain Jake say we need to build faith muscles?
8. Why was Harold such a sign of God's grace in Parker's life?
9. Were you surprised by Parker's unexpected inheritance? Why or why not?
10. How did Parker prove that he had been rehabilitated?
11. Why did Pastor Frank say we shouldn't compare our kiln's temperature to that of someone else's? (p. 95)
12. How did the Hamiltons and the Brooks become involved with each other?
13. How did Parker, Layton, and Brianne seek to disciple Gavin?
14. What did Pastor Frank say is the problem with trying to live *like* Jesus? (Chapter 32)

15. Brianne said the Christian life resembles living in a war zone. Explain her analogy.
16. How did Layton respond to Gavin's statement that he didn't deserve Brianne?
17. What did Parker's involvement with the Collins family after their tragedy reveal about his character?
18. What factors contributed to Parker's decision to move from The Sloan House?
19. What did Amy say is the hardest part of parenting? (Chapter 44)
20. Name someone who has been wounded by life but has left you a legacy of faith.

MEET THE AUTHOR

Dr. Betty Hassler loves to translate her forty years as a pastor's wife into true-to-life stories of families growing in their faith despite today's secular mindset.

Betty is an accomplished speaker, writer, and author of both nonfiction and fiction titles. She has co-written nine Bible studies and numerous articles for Christian publications. With seventeen years of experience in Christian publishing, she served as editor of two magazines with a combined distribution of 750,000 readers.

Betty has a bachelor of arts degree in English from Baylor University and a master's and PhD degrees from Southwestern Baptist Theological Seminary. She has served on church and association staffs and as a Christian counselor.

Now as a freelance editor and writer, she lives with her husband and near her two sons and grandchildren in northwest Florida. She loves practicing conversational English with international students and traveling.

Coming Soon from WestBow Press

A Glimpse *of* Mercy

Trophies of Grace Series

BOOK 3

Turn the page for an excerpt from Chapter One.

December 22

Holly Brianne Hamilton rested her chin on her younger brother's strawberry blonde head. Standing behind the sofa where he sat, she had a direct view of the Internet site on his iPhone. She reached past his shoulder and clicked on a pop-up menu.

"Hey, knock it off." Ty pushed her arm away.

"How'd you know it was me?" she asked in wide-eyed innocence.

"I wonder," he groused. Holly tousled his curls before settling into an armchair nearby. Tyler, or Ty as the family called him, seemed to have grown six inches while she was away at college for her first semester. With his mother's hair color and ocean blue eyes, plus his dad's height and build, he combined the best features of both parents. She had to admit Ty was *hot*—at least to girls who weren't his sister.

Holly couldn't believe he'd completed half his senior year of high school, and she'd barely heard a word about it. "Ty, don't you have any Christmas shopping left? Let's go somewhere."

He glared at her. "Not on your life."

She started to ask why, then remembered their most recent outing. Outside the food court at the mall, a girl Ty liked smiled in his direction. Holly took his arm possessively and steered him around a corner. Ty jerked free, but the damage was done.

Was it her fault the girl hadn't guessed they were brother and sister?

With her father's dark hair and eyes and her mom's petite form, Holly didn't resemble her brother. In more ways than physical, they were opposites. *Strange*, she thought. *Same gene pool.*

Apparently, Ty hadn't forgiven or forgotten the experience. Now, when she wanted to hang out, her prank had cost her his company.

Ty's phone rang. Quickly he clicked to answer. "Yeah ... Sure ... Sounds good."

"Who was that?" Always curious, Holly tried to get a look at the name.

"None of your business."

Holly took the rebuff in stride. Ty was a quiet, shy kid, who seemed to manage life with little interference from his parents or sister. His pensive moods often left her wondering what was going on in his thick head. On the other hand, she was a babbling brook, who daily regaled her family with elaborate accounts of her adventures.

Surely, I can break through that shell of his, she mused. She folded her arms resolutely. The Christmas holidays would be a good time to try and make a dent.

Meanwhile, her mind turned to more immediate concerns. Taking out her cell phone, Holly glanced at the time. "Has the mail come?" she asked in a loud voice to no one in particular.

Her mom peered around the corner from the kitchen. "Why do you want to know?"

Bounding to her feet, Holly gave her an agonized look. "For eighteen years I've suffered the cruel fate of a Christmas Eve birth. On the positive side, my nineteenth birthday is days away." She closed her eyes and dramatically held out her open palms to her mother. "Please hand over my deluge of packages, money, and gift cards."

Brianne Brooks Hamilton steered her daughter toward the kitchen island to survey her treasure trove, which she had carefully sorted into stacks. Holly fingered the cards, eyes still closed. The biggest one, no doubt from Holly's grandmother, Olivia Hamilton, would include a large, impersonal check. Her dad had already explained that his mother would be spending Christmas in Italy with his sister, Alexis.

Holly could count on one hand the times she had seen her Aunt Alexis in person. She was a little-known fashion designer whose long-term relationship with a wealthy Italian live-in had produced no marriage or children. Alexis would probably send her usual gift card packaged with a scenic picture of her draped across some gorgeous Italian landmark.

Holly looked through the other cards, mostly from family friends. The lone package was from Kyle Brooks, Grandpa Brooks' brother, who always sent something related to his years in the diplomatic corps. Exotic treasures, usually jewelry or cultural knickknacks, awaited her. Eagerly, she picked up the package.

Holly had the ability to take a present, shake and wiggle it, weigh it in her hands, smell it, listen intently, and invariably guess its contents. This talent lent a certain mystique to her reputation as an amateur sleuth.

"Simple curiosity will take you amazing places," she'd tell her friends. Ty called her a snoop, and her dad complained about her penchant for finding his chocolate hiding places. As Holly stood lost in thought, her mom snatched the cards and gift away and pretended to hide them in a cupboard. "You know not to open anything for two more days."

"Okay. At least I know they're in a safe *findable* place." Holly ducked before her mom swatted her with a kitchen towel. Her mom's laugh quickly turned into a nasty coughing fit. Holly grabbed a glass and filled it with water. Handing it to her, she studied her mom's slender frame. "That cough is awful. Shouldn't you take something for it?"

When the coughing subsided, her mom downplayed the incident. "I am. I had that respiratory infection right after Thanksgiving. Then, a week ago I caught a cold. My cough is the last mutinous villain to kill." She gave Holly a wicked grin.

Holly didn't look convinced. As she headed back to the family room, she said a silent prayer for her mom, who had a busy few days ahead. Family gatherings at Christmas were noisy, active affairs in the Hamilton/ Brooks households with plenty of food and festivities. The birthday girl frowned, wondering if her mom could handle it all.

Gavin Hollister Hamilton walked into the house from the garage and down the hall to his study. He threw his jacket on an armchair and deposited his briefcase next to the desk. Enticing smells from the kitchen drew him the way he'd come and right into the arms of his lovely wife.

"Aw, I thought I had sneaked in." He planted a kiss on Brianne's cheek.

She grinned, "You did, but I was lying in wait. Somehow, I just knew you'd head for the kitchen."

Gavin held her close. The two rocked silently back and forth. He might be a force to contend with in a courtroom, but his wife could sway him like a reed. Brianne had captured his heart at a time in his life when no one of her caliber should have cared about him, much less grown to love him.

"How did I get so lucky to be standing here hugging you?"

Brianne loosened his tie in a playful gesture. "Well … you had a mentor named Layton Brooks, who just happened to have a lovely daughter—that would be me. Besides, I worked for your brother at The Sloan House. A happy coincidence, don't you think?"

"Yeah, a chance meeting," he laughed. "The rest, as they say, is history."

Brianne rested her head on his shoulder. Gavin wondered for the millionth time how she could have fallen in love with a former alcoholic and drug user. He'd gotten clean largely through the efforts and prayers of his older brother, Parker, who had saved his life after an overdose.

Reluctantly, Gavin released his bride of twenty years. "Thanks again for loving me."

"It's a tough job, but …"

"Somebody's got to do it." They finished the sentence together.

"How're the kids?"

"Holly's obsessed with her birthday and Ty—well, he's just Ty. They're around here somewhere."

He led her into the kitchen where he opened the oven door, lifted the lids off pans cooking on the stove, and got his hand slapped. The usual.

Printed in the United States
by Baker & Taylor Publisher Services